I0772610

CASEY MASTERSON'S REVELATIONS OF THE RAVEN MASTER

VOLUME ONE

By Casey Masterson

POE BOY
PUBLISHING

Table of Contents

Dedication

For Nan – Thanks for taking that scared little thirteen-year-old under your wing. I owe it all to you.

Introduction From The Raven Master

The unkindness waits.

The Tower's torture chamber now serves to agonize apathetic students in day's transparency, bringing life and learning to a place that once dealt only in death. Yet, as night invades, the shadows of suffering regain their eternal reign. Monarchs may pass, the never-setting empire may wane, but the terrors of this room forever cling to the brick walls. Even in the day, when the dark of the past is curated into well-lit displays, the very air oppresses visitors with echoes of violence.

It is here that the nine ravens sit upon cases and artifacts, signs and plaques. Each eyes the Rack with cocked heads. The device is stationed at a slant with a glass covering its broad, wooden surface. Upon the glass cover is etched a human silhouette, splayed as a victim might be, though no mouth or facial features are given to represent its pain.

The Rack moves. A raven flaps its wings impatiently. It is not the actual implement in motion, as its mechanisms have long since rusted together, but the casing that disrupts the stillness, moving until it stands upright. A thud thunk of boots resounds from the opening. Each bird flies to the ground, hopping along the tile floor single file to meet their guide.

The Raven Master carries a lantern. He is attired much like his yeomen brethren, all of which have long since retired till duty awakens them at daybreak. His uniform is black, with red lining the edges, the frills of his great coat, and the emblem on his chest. His top hat is decked similarly. The marks of his trade, however, are not restricted to his attire. The true testament rends his face. The talon-marks sliced past his eye, and into his cheek. The wound has never healed. The ravens will often nip the meat from his face to keep the wound open. In some instances, bone protrudes.

The man turns and descends. His feathered companions flutter before him and scuttle behind. Only when the last raven arrives on the dirt pathway below does the trapdoor close behind them, returning the Rack to its former position. Their path is lined with bricks, littered with bones, and recedes into the earth. The only obstacle for the travelers is the occasional staircase. A corvid perches on their guide's shoulder and begins pecking at his eye. He only needs to swat at the air near her for the bird to desist.

The tunnel opens to a catacomb. Graves are etched into the walls. Their occupants sometimes spill a limb from their coffin. The walls extend farther up than the light can reveal, and the Raven Master knows most of the tombs are filled. Only a crevice at the wall's right end remains uninhabited, although some aspire to this status through their resident's disintegration. At the end of this cavernous gravesite is a door. It is high, wooden, barred with iron, and with rusted circular handles. When opened, a library beckons with the inviting scent of wax and tomes. This room is better lit than its predecessors, with candles sporadically mounted upon the shelves' sides. Cobwebs spread across the ceiling, between dark leather-bound books, and upon the candelabras.

The man drags his finger along each unmarked title. Some spines are more worn than others; they brandish their creases and scuffs with pride. A volume is selected. The ravens perch on the rooms' only piece of furniture; an armchair. It has a cherry wood base and a red leather covering, which is occasionally punctured along its rims. Cotton pokes out from some of these holes. Three ravens alight on the chair's back and three rest upon each of the chair's arms. One of them tweaks at a cotton protuberance from the chairs back before allowing it to fall to the floor. When their decrepit yeoman sits between them, each tilts their head to get a better look.

"It is our honor to serve you as you serve us." *These words flowed with practiced ease. They were nimble on the Raven Master's tongue, rolling off the tip and melding with the air.* "We have robbed you of your flight so that you might preserve our Nation with your presence. This is why you are read tales of our grief to satiate you, both in visions of the world denied and of our karmic repentance." *He opens the book and places a finger below the first word.* "Allow me, if you will, to begin our penance."

The unkindness croaks.

Hayfield Wilder (feat. Carson Cash)

Excerpts from *Darkest Rural Mystery* Script

. . . autopsy reports showed that the victim was in the later stages of decomposition, making it difficult to see exactly how she died. With that being said, the coroner was able to say that this woman likely suffered greatly . . .

. . . in a nearby deserted shed were signs of a temporary hide-out. Whoever stayed there left behind blankets, food wrappers, and books containing strange symbols that experts attribute to witchcraft . . .

. . . unsolved status of this case has not stopped internet speculation. Other mysterious disappearances in the area, along with the crime's brutal and occult symbols and relics, have led people to believe that a secret group of occultists may be responsible. r/creepy has many posts detailing reasons for this belief . . .

You know, "if it bleeds" isn't just a Stephen King anthology. It's an adage used by reporters to equate gruesome stories with public interest. I should know — that's how I make my money. No, I'm not a reporter. Sure, my job is less respected by the older generation, but it's the writing gig of the future.

I sit at my desk, my room an engulfing void behind me, my laptop a blinding force of light. Some part of me hears my door open and shut, but I don't acknowledge it until my office chair is at a forty-five-degree angle.

Jay is using his weight on the mesh-backed chair's plastic rim to lean me away from my work, work that *he* needs done. His silver chain necklace is dangling in my face. The urge to pull on it is strong, but I resist so that he does not let me fall. After all, the only thing between a concussion and myself is his grip on my chair.

"I never knew you could be an asshole *before* you opened your mouth. Seriously, Jay, I could call Guinness for that."

"Chill with the sass theatrics. I've got important shit to tell you."

I stare up at him. I have an incredibly unflattering angle of Jay's face, starting from his chin upwards. He can't have a much better angle either, seeing as he is looking from my forehead down. I tire of this distorted perspective quickly, and I shift my weight forward to put the chair back in its proper place.

"C'mon, I mean it!" He whines, shaking the mesh-back. "Open our email."

"Fine, sure, just get off of my chair." I open *Gmail* only after Jay relents. We — correction — *he* gets a lot of fan-mail. They range from the horny ramblings of fangirls (we get the most of these), to complaints, to suggestions, to trolls. A majority of it remains unopened. The monotony of ignored incomers is broken up with a single blue line. The bolded text says the email came from cicada3301@gmail.com (name Ci Cada) with !! HAYFIELD !! on the subject line. "Could you get anymore cliché? What is it, an ARG?"

"That's what I thought too. But look how many times it was sent."

'100' stands next to the name. "Oh Jesus."

"There are at least five of these chains, too, which gives us 500 of this shit. But that's not the interesting part." Jay shifts to grab the chair's arm, shaking it, causing me to sway side to side. "You gotta read it."

I smack his hand before I open the e-mail:

Darkened Theatre Productions (AKA Jay),

Hayfield County is cursed. Beware the woods. The Wilder lurks within. Beware beware BeWare beWARE BEwARE bewa re

"Well that's fucking weird." I scroll, glancing through each message. All of them say the same thing, with minute differences between them: sometimes things are spelled wrong, other times there are more or less bewares. "This has to be an ARG. Or at least a *copypasta*."

"Maybe. But with how random the errors are, I think it was done by hand, or at least certain sections copied and pasted in different ways."

"Uh-huh. So it *is* an ARG?"

"Whatever it is, it's weird. I think you should look into it all. Y'know, see what the Internet has to say about the Wilder, if there is anything weird about Hayfield, hell, see if the place even exists."

"Do you really want to engage with this… whoever this is?" I make a vague gesture to the computer. "What if they're just another *yayvideogames*?"

"Then they are. Still worth a shot." Jay kneels down at the chair's left side. "'Sides, even if it is boring, I know a great writer. She's spruced up even the steamiest shit to draw in views." He grabs the arm rest and begins shaking me back and forth again. "Think about it. I haven't seen *anyone* else talk about Hayfield. We got first dibs, we can control the story."

I sigh, flopping my head to the side to catch Jay's deep, pleading stare. He's selling the dramatic look, practically only seconds from clasping at my feet like a cartoon character. "Whatever. But if it turns out to be dumb, I don't want to give this more attention than it deserves. The last thing an unhinged person needs is clout."

Jay's smile rivals my screen's light. "That's my girl!" He stands, clapping a hand to the top of my head. It's demeaning and possessive, like ruffling a child's hair, but I let him get away with it. "Now, hop to it, kid." He claps his hands twice, but he's gone before I can sock him in the stomach.

That boy is lucky he pays me.

r/creepy Posted by u/2scary5me 5 days ago
Urban Legend?
Hey, I guess this is a long shot, but I wanted to see if anyone else

heard this story before? I remember sitting on my Pop Pop's porch in Hayfield NJ as a kid. You probably haven't heard of it if you're not from the area, it's microscopic. It doesn't even have its own exit on the parkway! Anyways, the sun was starting to go down and my Pop-Pop told me to get inside before the Wilder came to get me. He told me the Wilder was a demon who ate up little boys and girls who didn't come inside after dark or some shit. I asked my mom about it, and she said it was just a story to keep kids out of the Pine Barrens at night. To be fair, he could have been trying to scare me inside, but I thought it was weird they said Wilder and not the New Jersey Devil. Anyone hear anything about this?

mnmaholic 5 days ago
idk Ive heard of the NJD but never that. Their probably just fucking with you
2scary5me OP 5 days ago
*they're
thatoneguy 5 days ago
prolly making this up. SCP or creepypasta anyone? Very unoriginal...
stfu1234 3 days ago
Nah, that's some real shit. Check out Weird NJ and you'll see all sorts of shit about Hayfield

"So lemme get this straight. The Wilder's like a rip off New Jersey Devil?"

"Not even close." I pinch the bridge of my nose. "The Jersey Devil is New Jersey folklore. This is a secluded old wives' tale. I haven't found it mentioned anywhere outside of Hayfield."

Jay's leaning forward on the couch. If he moves any further forward he'll be sitting on the floor. His face is laced in concentration and his hands are clasped between his knees. I stand before him and stare at my phone, which contains the *Google Docs* of notes I took for this story. He has yet to read my notes for himself in all the years we have worked together. Jay says it's because he likes the way I explain things, but I know it's because he is a terrible procrastinator. Nothing gets done without my nudge. Have I mentioned that he's lucky he pays me?

"Let me dumb this down for you. I can only find testimonials here and there about the Wilder on *Reddit*, mostly in regard to adults scaring kids to obedience. There's a Wikipedia page, but there's not much there."

"So how do you know it's not en-jay-dee confusion?"

"The little info there is doesn't line up. The Jersey Devil is a cursed baby from the Leeds family. The Wilder doesn't have *any* backstory. They say it came with the woods."

"So what you're saying is there is a lot of wiggle room for interpretation."

"Seems like it."

Jay smiles. It's not his 'made-for-camera' one either. You know the look: the sociable, buddy-buddy smile that YouTubers push. I'm not a psychiatrist, but my guess is that's part of what pulls viewers in. Videos can feel like conversations between friends as they are often personable, trustworthy, and one-sided exchanges of information. But anyone can tell you more goes into it than that. Jay's smile tells me that his gears are turning. I know what he's thinking, because it's the same thing I am thinking: How can we get the most views out of this?

The straight-forward answer is clickbait. Jay's reliance on embellishment is what keeps me doing what I love. If it's self-serving, so what? Everyone benefits. The audience expects a story and we give it to them. Does it *really* matter if *every* detail isn't fact?

"There's more." I move to sit on the couch next to him. He turns eagerly to meet my gaze. "There are a few disappearances. The most recent one was in the 80's, but they stretch back much further."

"We probably need something more recent. Maybe we can make fake *Reddit* posts or…" He pauses, then smiles. Have you ever seen the original Grinch? I never knew a person could really smile like that. "Even better: We get us some Wilder footage."

"Who the fuck do you think you are? Tom Savini? A three-am-challenge style puppet will get us roasted alive."

Jay waves me off. "You don't *need* to actually see him. Think about the *Blair Witch Project*. We just need to get footage that implies he's there."

"Not a bad idea." I'm hopeless with editing. That's Jay's department. He was a film student in college, so he knows how to pull out all the bells and whistles. I give him a smile filled with cautious optimism. "I guess we can give it a shot."

"Atta girl." He shoots up from his seat, leaving the living room in favor of the kitchen. "This calls for a celebration. *Pepsi* and gin?"

"What are we? College students?"

"Sorry I don't have anything fancier for you, your Highness." Jay returns balancing four *Pepsi* cans, one glass tumbler, a plastic, blue cup, and a bottle of *Aviation*. Jay parcels out the drinks, and we clink our glasses. We toast before slipping into gin-induced debilitation.

r/newjersey Posted by u/pumpitup 265 days ago.

Creepy town

Anyone ever go to/drive by/stay at Hayfield, NJ? Maybe I was there too late at night, but this place just gives me bad vibes. I swear I've never seen black like between those trees. Those people are stuck in the past, I swear. The reception out there is so spotty. What if I got lost out there?

user1067532 264 days ago

Bruh since when does no reception == evil????

I didn't tell Jay everything I found out about Hayfield. I can see his reaction now: stunned silence then an uproar of laughter. In spite of what he'd have you believe on the channel, Jay thinks the supernatural is a part of the Barnum paradox: There is a sucker born every minute, so exploit them while you can. I'm the skeptic (I use that term liberally.) Don't lump me in with those teens in all black that swear by crystals, or the old hags that use witchcraft as an excuse for schizophrenic tendencies. I just think there is more to the world than what it presents to us.

Jay knows this about me. It's a fact that has been the butt of many jokes. That's why I didn't tell him about the twinges this town made me feel in my stomach. You know the feeling: the one you get when you do something wrong, when something *is* wrong? Your stomach shudders before the punishment, the killing blow. Or maybe it's all the gin I drank.

I wake up at threeish on the ground before the couch. My *Pepsi* concoction is dried on the carpet. Jay is asleep on the couch. His snores activate my headache. I drag myself to the bathroom but find my body refusing to throw up. I pull the trick beloved by eating disorders and the acid burns my throat. The sting of *Pepsi* reminds me I won't be able to drink that again for a few days without feeling nauseous. Taste can be a real bitch.

My room comes as a welcome change to the carpeted floor or leaning into the porcelain throne. I don't bother with the lights. I crawl into bed and plug in my phone. An old memory declares squatters' rights in my brain and refuses to leave. I squeeze my eyes shut in an attempt to silence the din of memory. It's a common fact that brains are bitchy as fuck when you are trying to sleep. Apparently, a prerequisite for REM is reliving every shitty memory you have.

Mine starts in the woods. There's a reason a lot of horror movies take place here. I don't know if it's the density of the trunks, height of the trees, or a general "fuck you" to anyone who approaches, but night becomes solidified in a forest. The dark is an entity. If it wasn't so foreboding, so cold, you might be willing to reach out and touch it. Another shitty part about the woods — day or night — is how many things are in it that want to kill you. Poison ivy, poison oak, spiders, huge ass bugs that have no business flying, snakes, bears… Okay, so bears probably don't come to campgrounds in New Jersey but cut me some slack. I was eight.

There were no bathrooms in our pop-up camper, but just down the packed dirt path was a bathhouse. My only weapon against the overburdening void was a thin ray of light. I shined it up toward the treetops. The leaves swayed in the nighttime breeze, their pale undersides ghostly against my harsh light.

The proverbial light at the end of the tunnel came in the form of the bathhouse bulb peeking from the darkness. It wasn't possible to see the full building at night, but the light illuminated the square face of the bathrooms. There was a privacy partition separating the men and women's bathrooms right in the middle. The light was fixed just above it.

I had that feeling you get in horror games you get when you need to go around a corner, but you also *know* there is something waiting on the other side. This fear plagued me often throughout my childhood. I would hide behind my dad as he unlocked the front door, only opting to enter the house once I saw he made it inside unscathed. This fear was amplified at God-knows-what-time at night without a dad-sized human shield.

It turned out there *was* something to fear behind the partition. A bug (*maybe* a beetle, but what eight-year-old is a certified entomologist?) played sentinel in the doorway. Its solitary march brought it to the middle of the entrance way. I really had to pee. At the rate it was going, I'd probably ruin my jammies before getting past the bug. With the bladder pressure rising, I do the only sensible thing I can think of and hop over it. It's a running, pole vaulter's effort, when all I truly need is a jump-over-a-crack style hop.

Bzzzzzzz.

The low thrum of the bug's wings may as well have been my swan song. I ran screaming in the opposite direction and secured the nearest stall door. Would the bug follow me? Would I be safe in the stall? Was I falling victim to the eight-year-old's impeccable sense for drama? None of these questions mattered to me, because I really had to pee.

I turned to face the toilet. My nose wanted to retreat. Even as an adult, I find it astonishing that people can't figure out how to keep stalls clean. All you have to do is aim the paper-wad into the toilet and flush. People are potty trained at, what, two? It's not rocket science. Maybe some people just enjoy leaving their mess to gross out others in a long-distance satanic ritual. The water was just under the brim with floating pieces of corn and *Hershey*-squirts marinating in the worst soup ever. Seeing as flushing would only cause the toilet to overflow, and the bug's buzzing was gone, I decided to change stalls. I attempted to slide back the lock, but it would not budge. I used my palm in an attempt to force it, and — *THUP.*

My reaction was louder than the noise itself. Something bumped against the door, and my allowance was on the bug. I hugged myself. I bit my lip. Then the toilet began to bubble.

Bzzzz. Thup thup.

I didn't know which way to look anymore, so I stood sideways. In front of me, something was constantly bumping against the stall door. Behind me was another huge beetle on the wall, and with another bubble from the toilet, a second one joined it.

The situation turned to over-stimulation city in .2 seconds. The *thup thup* against the door turned to *thump bam.* The toilet began to overflow, muddy water soiling my shoes. The waves came from the beetles flying up from the water and coating the wall. Surfing on these waves were a combination of maggots and worms, which tried

and failed to burrow into the tile. I'm stuck between all of this.
Bang
Bzz
Blub
C'mon, Maggie, think of something!
Bang
Bzz
Blub
Maggie, c'mon!
Bang
Bzz
Blub
"Maggie!"

My eyes tear open. The sudden silence makes the noise even more real for me. I must have dozed off in my reverie because the swarm is now replaced with filtered sunlight. The only danger now is the ever-impatient Jay at my door.

"Maggie, c'mooon!"

"Jesus, Jay, someone better be dying!"

This is taken as permission to swing my door open.

"Your ass'll be dying if you don't get ready to go ASAP. We've got some haunted woods to explore."

Carter Cash @ccash_YT · 14h
Ik you guys have been asking me to cover Darkened Theatre Productions for like ever

Carter Cash @ccash_YT · 14h
Honestly I dont think there is anything else to add. TRO had a super solid analysis on Jay/his team.

Carter Cash @ccash_YT · 14h
What it comes down to is I don't have anything new/exciting to add so I won't. You know my opinion already.

Carter Cash @ccash_YT · 14h
To make it up to you. I'll give you guys a sneak peak of what I'm putting together now.

I wish I could be as happy as the guy across the street. You can't
help but wonder what is going so well for a guy that is violently
swaying in time with the radio. Although I can't hear him, I can see
his raw joy from belting out what may or may not be his favorite
song. He even has a little head swivel going on. Meanwhile, I'm
staring ahead, probably frowning, thinking about how I'd rather be
traveling to Timbuk-fucking-tu than Hayfield. The world is such an
oddly fluid place. Car-Man and I can be at the complete opposite end
of the emotional spectrum at the exact same time. When the light goes
green, Jay turns right, and the dancing man drives straight out of my
life. My friend is too lost in trying to clap on beat to *Fitz and the
Tantrums* to acknowledge the once-in-a-lifetime solo performance of
the amateur musician in a soccer-mom van.

I wonder if I would ever recognize Car-Man if I saw him again.
Probably not. Some people are only meant to exist in certain places.
It's why you'd get so freaked out to see your teacher in the
supermarket as a kid. That's not her element. Car-Man's element is
grooving in his car, Jay's is behind the camera, mine is anywhere but
the woods. Our destination keeps dawning on me. I wish I could stay
in the dark.

"Hey, have you ever been down there?" Jay casts me a sideways
glance. He has given up his half-assed effort to clap along.

"Hayfield? I've never heard of it until the e-mail."

"I don't think anyone knows about Hayfield willingly." Jay
smiles, waits a moment to see if the joke lands (I snort), before
continuing. "I meant down in the Pine Barrens."

"I used to go camping down in Bass River."

"Don't you hate trees?"

I scoff. "I don't *hate trees*."

"Right. You're scared of the Jersey Devil and the Witcher —"

"Wilder," I correct.

Jay dismisses me with a wave. "Whatever. You're afraid of those
things."

"I'm more afraid of the bugs. You know, things that I'm *actually*
likely to run into?"

A red light presents Jay with the opportunity to raise his brows at me. "Yeah, sure. 'Cause bugs totally fly out of toilets."

I always regret telling him these things. I'm an idiot for thinking Jay'd do anything but turn my dream trauma into a joke. "Fuck you."

It's Jay's turn to snort now. "You wish."

Once upon a time, he may have been right, but he pissed on that flame a long time ago. If you were to ask me *why* we're still friends, I'd probably gape and stutter long enough for you to tell me to stop acting like a codfish. I know that deep down, somewhere in my cold, shackled heart, I must love him. Not romantically (gross), but like a skeleton in my closet I've learned to live with. And, sure, the fact that he pays me to do what I love doesn't hurt either.

"Seriously though, Mags, how's the script coming?" It is very like Jay to ignore my hurt, my cascade of emotions torrenting my thoughts in high tide.

"I haven't started yet."

"Seriously?" The accompanying look on his face threatens to reawaken the argument. "You're usually so on top of things."

"We're going there to get something filmed, Jay. I can't write if I have no idea what you're filming."

"You couldn't even come up with an outline?"

In Darkened Theatre Productions, facts tend to tailor to our ideas. That's our job as storytellers, right? We give the people what they want to hear. If the facts can't do that, it's our job to bedazzle the tale a little, keeping the views flooding in and the fans loyal to our choice content. This is why an outline shouldn't be too hard to pull off, but I'm not about to tell him I'm procrastinating off a gut feeling. That's just subjecting myself to a car ride length roast.

"I want to get whatever information we can get from the Hayfield locals first. A frame narrative of truth will do wonders for whatever you cook up." I give my best assuring smile. The best storytellers can put their hand on the Bible and swear by it. Maybe that's another reason why Jay and I get on so well. We have a mutual vow of silence; our embellishment remains *our* secret.

"This is why you get paid the big bucks, Mags."

I attempt to wave him off. It'd be bad for our *Tom and Jerry* dynamic if I gave into his charm so easily. Yet, I'm smiling, and so is he.

8,861,242 views Sept. 19, 2022 Sponsored: RAID Shadow Legends
...more
36,480 Comments

GamerInSpace - Sept. 19
It's a shame they have to resort to shilling BS for views. Feel kinda bad for what's her name. Kinda seems like Jay is using her talent.

MommyIssues - Sept. 19
      Thats what I was thinking. I feel like the episodes themselves are well written but they're just in poor taste.

GamerInSpace - Sept. 20
Agreed. Maybe she should try to do her own thing and see what she's capable of on her own?

Loser1998 Sept. 22
idk why the writer puts up with Jay. He seems like a prick. Try and do your own thing girl!

Darkened Theatre Productions Sept. 30
TRO, you did an awesome job on your video, but I think youre being a little unfair. Maggie and I are best buds. To insinuate I'm using her?? That really hurts.

GamerInSpace - Sept. 30
Oop someone is jealous his writer could be more successful.

Loser1998   - Sept. 30
Karma is a bitch I guess my dude rip. I wish her the best of luck!!!!

Darkened Theatre Productions - Sept. 30
Idk where you guys are getting the impression that Maggie
even wants to do this?? Love her to death but she would
freeze on camera. She does so well on YT bc we are a good
team.

Mommy Issues - Oct. 1
Way to neg your writer ig

Google Maps heralds Hayfield about five minutes after we pass the
sign. We only notice the mistake once the app makes its petulant
rerouting noise. You would think the unnatural road-sign green
would stand apart from the pine trees and shrubs. Hayfield is like an
embarrassing secret: hidden and best kept lost. And yet, as we circled
back, the sun glared off of the sign, making it impossible to miss,
although it was rendered illegible. In a show of divine mercy, a
shadow passed over the sign moments before it instructed us to make
the next right.

The town simply appears. It is immediately apparent the Pine
Barrens reign here in spite of Hayfield's presence. An off-brand
ShopRite (ie. *Shop-N-Go*), a gas station, a cute little Stephen-King-
esque diner, and the rest of the town are scattered in clearings devoid
of tree trunks. Cars, mostly trucks, are the only sign that people dare
to invade the forest's privacy. The roads, in true New Jersey fashion,
are littered with potholes.

Jay curses as a particularly bad one makes our car *thunk*. "Do you
want to get us checked in?"

I shrug. "Sure. You should get some b-roll while you're waiting.
This place screams spooky vibes."

Jay nods, touching his fingers to his temple in silent appreciation
of my intellect, before pulling into the ever-creatively-named
Hayfield Hotel. It should probably be a *m*otel, but I suppose even
small towns can make use of alliteration. The cracker box exterior
screams, "Use a blacklight before touching anything!" A neon open
sign flickers in the window. The front door is propped open with a
brick, leaving the screen door as the only barrier between the great
outdoors and the front office.

"If I'm not out in five, come in to make sure the owner didn't go all Norman Bates on me."

"Gotcha."

Jay is turned toward the back seat as I step out of the car. I see him lift his camera bag and fastidiously unzip its case. He treats that thing like an ancient relic, but hey, for that price, I would too. New Jersey's gravel-style dirt pop-rocks under my feet as I head inside.

The screen door has no handle. I simply encourage it forward with my finger until the barrier recedes enough for me to slip inside. The receptionist doesn't look up to greet me, completely avoiding any pretense that she is working. Her attention is transfixed on the world's deepest computer nestled between the front desk and a closed door. On the wall above the doorway is a shelf with assorted taxidermied birds. Her speakers project the baritone melody of Carter Cash's voice. You learn fast that each YouTuber, no matter the genre, has something that separates them from the others. Jay has his looks, *Lazy Masquerade* has his mask, and Carter Cash has his voice. It has the allure of a siren brandishing disturbing content at the rocks. He's a pretty private guy. As far as I know, Carter has never had a face reveal, the only option for fan-mail is e-mail in lieu of a PO box, and he never really engages with *YouTube* drama. He has his opinions of other creators, which I think is unavoidable, but aside from tweets, he does little else to address them.

The receptionist finally acknowledges my presence by pausing Carter's soliloquy about the ascensionist propaganda in *KanyeQuest*. When she looks up, I can tell this girl is trying to look much older than she is with inordinate amounts of eyeshadow. She passes the receptionist stereotype test, I'll give her that. "You want a room?"

I'm taken aback by her voice. How can someone so young sound like they've smoked eighty packs a day for forty years? "I think we should have a room booked."

"Nope." She makes no effort to check any log. "Nothing has been reserved."

"Are you sure?" The look on her face silently scolds, *yes, I am sure, and no, I'm not checking*. I sigh. This is what happens when you trust Jay to do something responsible: he doesn't follow through. I pull out my debit card from the rubber sleeve on the back of my phone. "You have any rooms with two beds?"

"Best I can do is one bed and a pull-out."

"That's fine."

As we wait for my payment to process, the receptionist casts Juliet-style pining glances to her monitor.

"You know," I begin. "*MamaMax* has a pretty good video on *KanyeQuest*. So does *Nexpo*."

"Uh-huh."

I consider telling the kid that the roof is caving in to see if it has a similar effect on her disposition, but she returns my card before I have the chance to experiment. She slides me two keys with blue rubber-protectors at the end. Both have the number four written on them in black Sharpie, although one is so smudged it almost looks like a nine. "Thanks."

"Uh-huh. Have a good stay."

Cash's voice beckons me back as I exit the office. Outside, it's what film and photography nerds like Jay dub "golden hour." The sun kisses the Earth with its shimmering aura. Everything, even the shade beneath the trees, seems to embrace the glow. Jay, lost in his digital eye, rivals Apollo in his radiance. His dirty blonde hair is practically a part of the light.

The mechanical eye suddenly whirls around to focus on me. "And here we have our shit-shack, starring our very own shit-show, Margaret Costello!"

I flip him off as I make towards our room. I can hear Jay rushing to follow behind, rocky soil screaming beneath his stride. The key slides into its slot, but before it can turn, the door pulls inwards. There is someone in the doorway to greet us.

JAY

r u ready?

why tf are you texting me?

you're literally in the next room

srry busy packing

just getting my bag togther

what time is check in?

what

did you seriously not book a room???

on it now

ugh okay

Fast forward five minutes. The towel boy is sitting on the bed, head tilted back, a once-white washcloth stopping the blood flow. Jay has yet to stop laughing and I have yet to stop feeling guilty. His punishment for a cheap *jumpscare* was a right hook to the face. If I had let him explain, I'd know he was just prepping the room for the next guest. The dropped linens, now sprinkled with blood, lay in the doorway as evidence. I'd also know that this faux-intruder is Carter Cash.

I recognized his voice from his first utterance, but he only confirmed my suspicion when Jay's buffering perception caught on minutes later. Apparently, he helps his parents out at the hotel when he isn't terrifying *YouTube*'s audience.

"Again, I'm really sorry. Can I get you ice or..?"

"'Sokay, really."

Something tells me I could have stabbed him in the face and I would get a similar response.

Jay is less endeared. "Not for nothing, man, but what were you expecting to happen? Creeping around in someone's room is asking for an ass kicking."

"Soph wasn't supposed to rent this room out. I haven't finished cleaning yet." Carter was a lot shorter than I expected him to be. Maybe it is the deep voice, but I expected him to be at least nine feet tall and hulking in stature. Instead, he was a guy with average build and raven ringlets managed with gel. His dark eyes give the impression of a deep and soulful romantic interest from a YA novel.

"Ignore him," I advise my victim. "He can be a dick."

Jay doesn't defend himself. Carson simply shrugs and removes the towel from his nose. Blood has thankfully stopped gushing like Vesuvius down his face. "What brings you guys to Hayfield anyways?"

"What's it to ya?" Jay's eager to fight.

The other YouTuber won't take the bait. "No one comes to Hayfield for the fun of it." He leans forward in a conspiratorial fashion I can feel my friend roll his eyes at. "I bet you're here for the Wilder."

"What can you tell us about it?" Jay nudges me as I speak, but I'm not about to pass up information for my script.

"I'll be honest, I'm a little hesitant to talk to you guys about it. You know, in light of the circumstances."

"Because Maggie punched you in the face?"

"No." Carson leans back. "I *literally* just posted that I was looking into local urban legends. I knew you liked extorting facts, Jay, but I didn't think you'd resort to copying me."

Jay inserts himself between Carson and me. I grab one of his arms. I don't think he'd hit the already injured man, but Jay isn't above seizing the dramatic moment. "Like fuck I did! Listen. People make stories about the same thing *all the time*. If we are doing the same thing, then who cares? I bust my ass editing and filming these videos, and she puts her heart and soul and blood and whatever the fuck else she can into those scripts."

Carson nods. "I have no doubt you work hard. All I'm saying is this is a bit too coincidental. Honestly, Jay, maybe if you didn't build a reputation as a liar, it'd be easier to believe you."

"If my audience wanted fast facts, they'd go to *Wikipedia*. My job, *our* job, is to entertain." He motions back to me. "When it comes down to it, we are storytellers."

"At the expense of your audience's trust and the story?"

Jay, instead of turning this room into a crime scene, whirls on me. "Are you *really* going to let him say this shit about your writing?"

I've been pacified by the fact that I punched this man in the face. The last thing I deserve to give him is a verbal lashing. But now, it looks like stepping in is the only thing preventing Jay from going Travis the Chimp style apeshit (chimpshit?) on Carson. "You're right, Carson. We do embellish a little, sure, but isn't it just as important that these stories be told? Like Jay said, if the audience wants facts, they can look them up. The least we can do is try to stir interest."

Jay nods along like one of Plato's dutiful students. Carson looks a mixture of miffed and disappointed. My guess is he thought I was his only chance to talk sense into Jay, and he lost it. He shakes his head in a "not mad, just disappointed" style as he pushes off of the bed. "Whatever helps you sleep at night."

The YouTuber's receding footsteps are matched with Jay's smug silence. He thinks we won this battle, but I'm not so sure. The difference between Jay and me is that I *know* this is unethical. Misinformation about urban legends is one thing, but I've written speculation on everything from disappearances to unsolved murders. Jay convinces himself that all he does is right and should be adored by all. I don't know where he gets the rose-colored blinders or the drink of delusion, but the pain of collusion is dulled by passion. I just want to write. If I have to compromise my morals to do it for a living, then so be it. All I'm doing is writing a sort of metafiction.

"Hey, Maggie, it's all good." Jay mistakes my silence for melancholy. I don't correct him. "I think your scripts are great. Everyone enjoys the content. Remember that whole phase *YouTube* went through trying to get you your own channel?" He places a hand on my arm. "Just don't let that prick get you down, okay?" There is a therapeutic look washed over his face. This is another look that's not for the cameras or for the audience: it's just for me. Maybe that's why I love him. Even when he misreads me, he thinks he knows how to help.

The first time we met, I was crying. I can't remember why, but God knows I had enough reasons to in college. I was sitting on a bench, hands wringing one another, tears eroding my cheeks to form red deltas. I don't even remember where he came from, but soon, Jay was beside me. I didn't know him, and he didn't know me, but barriers like this don't matter to people like him. He sat beside me, told me everything would be alright, and offered me an undesirable hike to get my mind off things. Cue lifelong friendship. Jay is a lot of things. An idiot, an asshole, and one of the most caring people I know. That makes all of his insufferable traits bearable. Almost.

"Yeah, okay."

Jay ushers me into a hug I don't reject. Say what you will about Jay McCloud, but he invented the bear hug. "I know what'll make you feel better."

"Oh yeah?"

"Let's go get some night footage."

He's off the mark, as always, but like every time before this, I agree anyway.

r/horror Posted by u/earthdemonbmine 4 years ago

Random Fears

Are you guys ever afraid of places when you have no reason to be? I'm afraid of Ikea. Idk something about getting lost in there just freaks me out. Like, I have no reason to be afraid (I've never even been there.) Fuck, I don't even think there is a store near me. Is it symbolic or am I just an idiot? Idk.

This is the part of the horror movie where you yell at the characters to go home. It's stupid to waltz into the woods, you yell. This is suicide in any woods-based flick: only this isn't a movie, it's my life, and the only thing screaming is my internal monologue.

God, I hate the woods. I hate them almost as much as I hate Jay dragging me here without a peep of objection from yours truly. He's ahead of me now. I can tell he is in his artistic zone by the way he is hunched forward, as if good content is something he can pounce on. His camcorder swivels from side to side to take in our surroundings. The trees pose. The forest plots. All Jay can see through his lens is monetization. This is the stuff that horror fans live for: eerie, quiet, ethereal beauty with a dark overtone.

I'm stuck with the flashlight. Actually, that's inaccurate. I *insisted* that I carry the flashlight in case I need to hit someone with it. The light should make me feel better, but the woods have the tactical advantage. The darkness and the trees signed a peace treaty long ago. Thick canopies, overpopulated grasses, and dense trunks provide a safe house for darkness from the subtle assault of the moon's rays. In turn, the darkness hides the wood's nefarious activities. The pitch is thicker in the forest and it oozes between wooden fingers.

"Don't you have enough footage?"

Jay's attention snaps back fast. His camcorder snaps to his side, his eyes prep for a sarcastic roll, and his lips press together. "Did you *really* just talk while I'm filming?"

"Jay, this is b-roll. You're just going to mute it and slap stock horror music overtop anyways."

There goes the eye roll. His pupils go in slow motion, exaggerating his exacerbation to the fullest. I'm not in the mood to counter with a witty retort. "It's freezing out here. I just want to go back to our room and sleep."

"Then go back. I wanna get more footage, but I'll be done soon."

I raise my brow. "You want me to leave you out here, alone, without a flashlight?"

He lifts his camcorder from his side and sways it to and fro. "I got a light. And night sight."

"Let me rephrase. You want *me* to walk back *alone*?"

"Chicken?"

"Hell fucking yes I'm chicken! You know I hate it out here."

"Right, 'cause of that camping trip." He brings his camcorder up to record our surroundings once more. "What happened again?"

"Nothing. I just don't like being out here at night. It's freaky."

Jay studies me. Obviously, I don't know what he is thinking, but I can see the gears turning. "I'll walk you to the hotel. But I *am* coming right back. I just need to find something good."

"Like *what* exactly?"

"Hell, I don't know. Movement in the bushes. A trespassing sign. *Abandon all hope ye who enter here* carved above a cave." As he speaks, he turns and starts heading toward town. I follow at his side. I dip the light upwards, scanning the bottom of the leaves above us. The undersides are specters of the chlorophyll on their upper skin.

"It'll probably be easy to catch a squirrel fucking about in the bushes or something. Then I can edit sound over it and *bam*, we have ourselves a Wilder."

"I guess." It's hard to be annoyed at him for wanting to stay out when he sounds so excited. "I can hold out for a little while longer. I mean, if you think you're close to stumbling on something?"

"Nah, it's okay. I get it, Mags."

I nod. I soon get lost looking at the ghosts above us. Jay, as far as I can tell, is concentrated on the path ahead. Gravel and sticks snap, crackle, pop below us. That is until he stops. I don't notice at first, since I'm looking upwards, so he's forced to grab my arm.

"You hear that?"

Now I am straining to hear against the forest's cacophony. Crickets sing. Wind whistles. Somewhere in the distance, a frog croaks. Jay screams. I scream. I flail around my flashlight, hoping to make contact with whatever scared my friend. My terror is interrupted by laughter. Jay's laughter. The situation dawns. I am no longer afraid of the darkness as wrath ignites within me. "Oh, you asshole!"

"I'm sorry, really, but you should've *seen* the look on your face!"

I punch him in the shoulder. I'm already walking away as he rubs the scorch mark I leave behind.

"Wait! Maggie, come back!"

"Fuck you!"

"No, really, I'm sorry!"

"No, *really*, fuck you!" The rush of internal flames drowns out anymore of his responses. I'm fortunate enough for my brazenness not to wear off until I reach the first lamppost.

In order to get back to my room, I have to pass the front office. Instead of YouTube commentary, I can hear music playing softly from inside. It's too low to make out the song, but I can hear Carter humming along. He's at the counter, flipping through the guest book. Although I snap my attention away, I can feel his eyes move onto me. The last thing I need right now is another confrontation. I'm already liable to say something vicious because of Jay, and my partner-in-crime has always been better at confrontation. Yet the footsteps are approaching, and there is no polite way I can think to say, "fuck off, I don't want to argue right now," so I guess this is happening.

"Maggie." Yup, it's definitely happening. I spin around to greet him, and Carter stops a respectful distance away. "Can you talk for a minute?"

"I guess. I'm pretty tired."

"It won't take long, I promise."

I cross my arms over my chest. "Okay, shoot."

"I'm sorry I lashed out at you guys earlier." This is refreshing. Jay only apologizes in a perfunctory manner. Societal norms need to call for an apology, or he needs to be caught red handed. "I guess I was worked up from the punch in the face—"

"Sorry again."

"No, I get it. I would've been spooked too. But it was seriously uncool of me to talk to you both like that. We have different ways of doing things, but I shouldn't hold that against you so seriously."

My lips tug to one side as if someone has begun sewing at the corner. "Look, Carson, I also get it. Between you and me, I can see why people get so pissed. Part of having a platform means having trust, and abusing it for clout isn't cool."

The YouTuber is silent for what seems like an uncomfortably long time, but is probably only thirty seconds. "You *do* have talent, Maggie. There's a reason people believe the stuff you guys put out, and it isn't Jay's delivery—"

"Watch it," I snap. "That's my friend."

"Right. What I meant was… I don't know. Maybe you should *try* writing an honest script, maybe about this, maybe not. I think you'll surprise yourself. Besides, reality will always have you beat, regardless of what sick stuff you can come up with."

"Maybe." I cast a glance over my shoulder. "Look, Carson, I really am tired."

He raises his hands like I have a gun to him. "Say no more. Sleep well."

We part ways mutually. Carter goes back to his books and I go to the room. Before I crawl into bed, I pull out my laptop and start typing: You picture a small town and you picture Hayfield, New Jersey…

I escape the swarm in the bathroom. I can't figure out how I managed this, but I know that the bathhouse is a distant memory to be washed away by the present. Now, I run.

The camper isn't that far from the bathhouse. In fact, I can just make out its porch light through the trees. It never gets closer. All of my surroundings look the same; Looming sentinels, darkness that threatens to pour through my eyes and down my throat, rocks rebounding from my kicked-up heels, pinging against my legs, the screaming of wind.

No, not wind.

It sounds like a cry. A caw, perhaps? Either way, it's getting closer.

The bird's strike is silent in spite of the build up. Each of its claws are the size of my feet. Any sound I make is drowned out by the birds SCREE. It brings me up into the air. Any kicking I do only drives me forward and back in an arc, causing the talons to dig deeper into my shoulders. Below, I see my camper. The porch light is a star from this height.

The bird lets go.

Eagles are known to drop turtles on rocks for easier eating. Is this the same idea? Will I split open when I crash against the camper? Will parts of me go everywhere? Or will I end up like the Robert Wiles' Sleeping Beauty, with the camper's roof morphed around my outwardly preserved body? Before I can find the answer to any of these questions, it all goes black.

I *jumpscare* myself awake with my own screams. The room is still dark, but I can make out my second shock once my eyes adjust: the pull-out couch is still folded up. And empty. I look at the tableside alarm clock.

3:30.

Where the fuck is Jay?

You picture a small town, and you picture Hayfield, New Jersey. They're one in the same. The trees are more populous than people. They stand like silent sentinels over general store and house alike. It seems like something out of a novel, but if you pinch yourself, you'll find you're not dreaming.

Only at night does this dreamy hideaway morph into a nightmare. The sheltering shade becomes a searing shadow. The void calls out from between its guards. They might not be the only things watching you either. Somewhere between the call of the wild and the allure of danger lies the focus of this video… The Wilder.

If I was a character in a horror story, my decision to return to the woods would be a good indicator of my imminent demise. This is the only other rule that should have been added to Randy Meek's survival guide: Never walk into the woods alone.   The only characters who get a 'get-out-of-death-free card' are final girls, but I don't think I would have what it takes to complete what James A. Janisse calls the Final Girl Circuit.

Yet here I am. I only have a flashlight, my phone, and the heaviest thing I could find in the hotel room. I never thought the surprise-inside-the-nightstand Bible would be so useful. Thanks, I guess, Jesus.

The worst part of the woods at night is the silence. Even the discord of cicadas and crickets is missing, so the only sounds are the ones I have brought along with me. I don't call out for Jay. If there *is* a Wilder, then it would come right to me. Leaves and twigs crunching beneath my feet are my sole contribution to the forest symphony. My flashlight serves as a beacon for moths and other flying insects, which remain undeterred when I swat at them with my tome. The swarms only get worse as I wander farther away from civilization's glue traps and *Bug-A-Salts*.

I'm way past the point I last saw Jay. Not that I can make out a discernible landmark, but I figure I've been walking way longer than earlier. This isn't too surprising; Jay was itching to find his own cabin in the woods or *Blair Witch Project* style murder house. Our audience expects more than a photoshopped Wilder hiding behind a tree or lurking in the distance, or whatever cheap scares could be pulled from the *Something Awful* forums. We pay our bills with imitative authenticity. Jay's probably looking for something tangible. Unfortunately, the only tangible things I can find are tree trunks and the thick cloud of darkness.

He's probably lost. The reception out here sucks ass in the worst way possible, so it'd make sense if he couldn't *Google Maps* his way out of the forest. What's really concerning me is that I can't make out the light of his camera anywhere. True, it would serve as a poor marker in advanced darkness, but I should at least be able to see a twinkle.

And then I find his camera. I kick it mid-step and the screen winks to life before going dark once more. My back tightens and my skin feels like someone threw hot and cold water on it simultaneously.

"Jay?" I ignore my previous reservations about speech. It may have seemed like a target on my back before, but if he is in *real* danger, how can I *not* call out to him? Something compels me to stay still in the hopes he can orient himself to my location. But what if he *can't* move? What if he's stuck someplace, or hurt, or swallowed by the forest like Kris Kremers and Lisanne Froon?

No. No no no. That's something that only happens in *Nexpo's Disturbing Things from Around the Internet* or *ReignBot's Stories from Our Disturbing World,* or our channel, or in fiction. This doesn't happen to normal people… except it does and that's why channels like ours thrive. What did Carson say? *Reality will always have you beat, regardless of what sick stuff you can come up with.*

I shine my light off the trail. Something is hanging from a tree branch. It's tied to the twig with cloth like a stereotypical hobo bundle. I move through the brush and persistent branches latch onto my clothes and skin in an attempt to save me from perceived danger. The bundle is black. I try to slide it off the branch, but its hold disintegrates at my initial touch. I point the light downward and the tingle returns to my skin. I reach down to grab the fallen object: Jay's necklace. Its silver luster is dulled by a coating of blood.

221-233-2710

i don't know what your hesitation is man

This is going to be good for you. Lessen the risk of losing your safety net.

Seriously. We'll be an awesome team.
We just got to do this.

Bruh no need to spam I had to pee

don't worry, I'm still game

I guess I get my own Final Girl Circuit after all. I know, I know, it's a horrible time to joke, but I need something to pull me away from the precipice of panic. It's startlingly simple to get out of the woods. My sense of direction isn't great, but any idiot can recognize that the glow and hum of a hotel sign means civilization. Horror movie logic dictates that slamming on guest doors is pointless. Let's not forget that this is New Jersey. Someone is more likely to throw open their door, tell you to shut the fuck up, then lock up once more. Luckily, there are people who are paid to attend to distraught hotel customers.

The lights of the main office are off, and the front door has abandoned its partnership with the brick to close up for the night. I almost give up hope, but I can make out a faint crackle of light from the back room. I slam the side of my fist onto the front door, causing the screen to rattle behind it. By the time I see a silhouette fill the small, rectangular window, I am practically punching the doorway.

Carter approaches with hands half raised in a plaintive manner. The neon sign shines a green haze over his face. He has yet to rub sleep from his eyes and he has a faint trickle of drool at the corner of his mouth. "Bit late for room service, huh?"

"Jay's gone."

The sandman's influence disappears. He throws the door open wide, motioning me inside. Carter flicks on the lights as soon as he finishes closing the door and ushers me into the back. It seems as though the lights in the building are connected, as the area is already lit before we step into it. There is a couch with a blanket thrown over the cushions and a recliner. Both look like they were pulled from someone's house after years of use. Across from the furniture is the world's deepest TV (which must have been bought in tandem with the computer). Along the far wall is what could legally pass as a kitchen area, with a counter, *Keurig*, and mini-fridge. The wall closest to the door boasts a wooden cabinet stripped of its doors. An assortment of books, magazines, and games litter the shelves. I put the Bible on a shelf and look up. Perched at the top of this makeshift-library is a taxidermied hawk. Its talons are digging into a branch, and its beady eyes are fixed on distant prey.

"That bird's freaky."

"She's a red-tailed hawk," Carter corrects. He crosses to the mini-fridge. "You don't like birds?"

"I grew up by the Shore. Birds mean beachside harassment."

Carter nods, pulling a water bottle from the fridge and the blanket from the couch. He drapes the latter over my shoulders and presents me with the former. "Take a seat, breathe, and tell me what's going on."

I nod my thanks and sink into the armchair. I feel a spring break beneath me. The YouTuber takes a seat on the couch and leans forward with his arms on his knees. I take a swig of water that I didn't realize I needed so badly before I tell him everything. Carter remains silent with the occasional nod. At the end, I present him with Jay's necklace. My confidant takes it and turns it over in his hands. Jay's blood streaks across his palm. Most of it is already soaked into my pocket, but a few of the crevices hold a morbid oasis between them.

"Here's what we're going to do. I'm going to go with you into the forest, and we are going to find Jay."

I blink in surprise. "Shouldn't we call the police?"

"Here's the thing, Maggie." He leans forward to hand me the necklace. "I think he's probably fine."

"But—"

"That's fake blood." I open my mouth to retort, but Carson cuts me off. "I get it. This is a scary situation and you got freaked out. But look closer at it. It's way too red and watery. It should be darker and congealed."

I furrow my brows. "So… This is just for show?"

"I'd guess so."

"I didn't see him bring any fake blood."

"The greatest magicians don't reveal their secrets. Same rule applies here, I'd guess. Your friend is a showman. He probably wanted to surprise you, set up a stunt, and got lost somehow. You've got to admit, that was *really* a cinematic find."

He has a point. I mean, if someone *really* wanted me to find it, why not just leave it at our door? And if it was part of something sinister, why would they take the time to set it up? "You really think he's just lost?"

Carter nods. "That, or he could've taken a nasty step somewhere. The ground is super uneven. Walking around in the dark is just asking to fall."

I return the nod. "So, we should look for Jay ourselves, so we don't make a big deal out of nothing. I get that. But if we can't find him—"

"If we can't find him, we come back here and hit the panic button behind the desk. The cops'll come right away."

I stand from the chair. "If we find him, you may need to press that button anyways."

Carter raises a brow. "Why's that?"

"When I find him, I'm going to kill him for scaring the shit out of me."

Red-Tailed Hawks Hunting
Found this video on YT and had to share. Apparently, these hawks hunt in pairs? That shit's wild.

"I hate the woods." I don't look at Carter when I say this so that our surroundings can feel the full brunt of my scorn. The trees have just started to thicken around us, once again leaving the hotel's light as a specter in the distance. It's somewhere close to four in the morning now. The darkness is unforgiving: asserting its dominance before the sun forces it back to the shadows.

"You picked an awful place to cover then." I didn't even need to look at my companion to see him shrug. The light shifted upwards on the path next to me before settling back down. In spite of the optimism Carson displayed before, he holds his flashlight like a spear he is ready to throw. The butt of it rests just on top of his shoulder and his fist is gripped in the middle of its handle.

"Jay picked it."

"Gotcha." Carson turns his head to look at me, but quickly looks straight ahead when he nearly blinds himself with the light. He squeezes his eyes shut to spare his vision. "What don't you like about the woods?"

"I don't know. I had a bad camping trip when I was little. I guess it left its mark."

I can see Carson frown. Before he looks over at me, he lowers his flashlight. "Something bad happen?"

"That's the thing. *Nothing* bad happened." I suddenly feel cold. I wrap my arms around myself. "I was walking in the woods at night, right? Maybe it was because I was so little, or the dark, or this huge bug I ran into but… I don't know. It just sort of ruined the vibe for me."

"Fear isn't always grounded in reality."

I look over to Carson to find him nodding sagely. "But to be afraid when *nothing* happened at all?"

"The woods were scary long before they were in any horror movie, Maggie. It's dark, full of bugs and animals, it's —"

The forest cries. Both of us freeze.

Carson raises his flashlight again, as if he is prepared to javelin the sound from the air. I realize I have nothing but my cell phone on me: bad choice for a weapon.

The forest wails again. Only this time, since we expect it, it's not an indiscernible howl. Sure, it's drawn out and filled with an emotion I've never before experienced, but I can make it out this time. *Help.*

"Jay!" I am moving before I can process where I intend to go. I can hear Carson calling after me, the thrum of his footfall as he tries to keep up, but I ignore him. I'm pure adrenaline. I can't usually run without pain in my hip and squeaky breath but I do it anyways. Any doubts I have are drowned out with another cry for help. I ignore the twigs and thorny brush snapping against my body and keep running.

I can't ignore the sudden precipice. Through moonlight and vaguely adjusted eyes I can see the rocky sides of this drop-off. I can't make out a bottom without Carson's light, but the tops of trees shimmer in the moon's radiance not far from the lip of the opening. I try to think about how tall the average tree is until my thoughts are interrupted by a hand on my back. I imagine it's Carson, because the collar of my shirt is pulled in a fist behind my neck, pulling my t-shirt against my neck, but the grip doesn't pull me to solid ground.

I think I can make out movement to my left, but my gaze is kept forward by something metal and cold pressed to my back.

"I'm sorry, Maggie." The voice is calm and comes from behind me. I can't turn to see him, but I know it is Jay who says this.

Before I can respond, I hear the shot and fall. I don't know why I don't feel pain. Why can I see? Why am I alive? I am falling. The ground is rushing closer and something warm is trickling down my back and front and everywhere. I'm going to die I'm g…

Darkened Theatre Productions @dtp_yt I don't know where to begin. Maggie was always better with words. Needless to say, I'll be on hiatus for a while.

Darkened Theatre Productions @dtp_yt Donate to Maggie's folks to help with the search. Link is in my bio.

Darkened Theatre Productions @dtp_yt Love you, Mags. Miss you every day. Please come home.

Carter Cash @ccash_YT · 14h I can not imagine the grief and devastation felt by Jay over at @dtp_yt. I met Maggie when she was shooting what was supposed to be an upcoming video on the Hayfield Wilder. She was very talented and bright.

Carter Cash @ccash_YT · 14h After he has time to process this, @dtp_yt and I will investigate this tragedy. Hopefully, we can bring out the truth, bring her home, and bring light to whatever *real* horror is in the Pine Barrens (because it's not the Wilder.)

Rain

Thick raindrops poured upwards as Melanie stared into the abyss above her.

At least, she thought they did. Another look to the sky proved that this was merely an illusion, as now she saw only the clear August sky above her.

Melanie felt like laughing at herself, though she would do no such thing, thank you. She was far too concerned with her image to look like a crazy person. Melanie was the kind of woman everyone loved to hate. She could ruin someone's life with a single catty comment and took pleasure in doing so.

Mel, the name by which only a select few cronies could call her, leaned against the railing of *Adventure*. The brand-new cruise liner was large enough to make the Titanic look wimpy. The newspapers had made a big fuss about the ship leaving port. Tickets sold out fast, but that was not a problem for Melanie. Much like entitled customers who complain to the manager, she always got what she wanted. The wind on deck was fierce and threatened to muss up Melanie's hair. A few loose strands of golden hair snapped like whips to ward it off before falling perfectly back into place. The laws of physics do not apply to beautiful people. If it *did* apply to them, well, not even the author of this piece would be stupid enough to point out Melanie's hair was getting frizzy.

Her *Venus* strapless sundress swayed majestically in the breeze, as clothing on popular people in teen movies often do. It was dark blue, with fancy fringes at the bottom. Her toes curled against the bottom of her matching sandals in an effort to guard against the breeze.

A pair of arms wrapped around her waist and someone kissed the side of her head. "There you are! I thought you were going to meet me after you had a drink with your girlfriends?"

Melanie turned to face her husband, Ralph. He was thirty years her senior, but he had deep pockets and a generous nature. She was more than happy to play wife until he met his end. Whether it was natural or not would depend on how much he bugged her for annoying things like affection.

"I was on my way to find you," she lied. At least, she thought she was lying. All she could remember were the raindrops that she refused to believe were real. If they really were just an illusion, why were they the only thing she remembered? She refused herself the trouble of worrying about it too long.

She placed a gentle hand on his *Tommy Bahama* Hawaiian shirt to push him back a little, which prompted her husband to drop his arms from around her waist. Ralph had gray hair that was balding towards the back. He was sensitive about it, which meant that Melanie brought it up often. Ralph's feelings of embarrassment over his follicle deficiency made her more confident about her own looks. His appalling shirt was complemented by his cargo shorts and sandals. He smelled like *Coppertone*. The source was displayed by the little bit of white left on his nose. Being married to Ralph made Melanie happy there were so many guys who were not Ralph that would just die for a romp in the sheets with her.

"Would you like to get a drink and sit by the pool?"

"Not really. I wanted to check out the club down below. Some of the girls are meeting up there." Melanie didn't know this to be true, but she wanted to be away from the old man she was stuck with.

Ralph gave a sad look that would be enough to melt the heart of the coldest ice queen. "It's just that… I haven't seen much of you this whole cruise and it's our honeymoon. I was hoping we could have fun *together* rather than apart."

Melanie's heart was made of dry ice, impervious to Ralph's attempt at pity. Still, if she were to get drunk, she wouldn't feel so bad about being with him. "Fine."

Ralph smiled and led his wife over to the tiki-bar. It had a grass skirt around the perimeter, covering the bar about three-fourths of the way. Only the bottom of the polished wood was visible through the jungle of bar flies' feet. Torches lit every corner and a coconut tip jar sat before the blender. A sticky note on the side declared "You must be trippin' if you aren't tippin'!" Most customers had the courtesy to not be trippin' regardless of whether the drinks were inclusive. The cruise line was hard to blame for the tacky decorations. Much like Ralph, a lot of the passengers seemed to give in to the tropical theme.

Melanie was above that cliché garbage.

Tropical drinks were featured on the menu, including favorites like *Malibu* bay breeze and sex on the beach. The bartenders were also encouraged to promote their own specials, such as mango tsunami and lei on the beach. The latter came in a souvenir turtle cup with flashing rainbow eyes. What the turtle had to do with the awful pun was irrelevant. It was just meant to be fun, and fun it was, as the turtle-shaped cocktail had enough alcohol in it to put a hardened drunk into a coma.

Something about the stupid little smile engraved into the plastic turtle made Melanie feel uneasy. It seemed to mock her. She decided to ignore this stupid feeling of dread and simply avoid that drink for now.

Ralph squinted to see the menu hanging at the back of the bar. "I'll take… a Miller Lite, please. What do you want, Mel?"

"Mango Tsunami."

The bartender nodded and handed the elder man his beer as he got ready to make her drink. The nametag exclaimed its owner's name was Tyler. He was just the kind of guy Melanie would find acceptable to flirt with while her husband was not paying any attention. Maybe she could slip away from Ralph and catch him when he got off his shift.

"You guys better enjoy the sun while you can," Tyler warned. "I heard we might be heading into a storm later on."

"I should've known," Ralph responded. "My knee always acts up when a storm is coming, right, honey?"

Mel gave an uninterested noise of agreement. She was more interested in watching Tyler shake her cocktail. When he handed the drink to her, she stroked his finger with hers before taking it. His hand withdrew quickly, and he moved to help another guest.

She liked it when people played hard to get.

As they walked away, Ralph looked over to Melanie. "Are you upset about the rain?"

"No." Her clipped answer hardly showed how strange she felt. Something about the storm seemed to give her the shivers. Maybe it was the correlation to the illusion she'd had earlier. Maybe it was because she hated the thought of being stuck inside with Ralph. It put them that much closer to being alone in the cabin together.

"I still think we'll make it to Tonga okay, as long as we don't have to sail too far around the storm. I know you don't want to miss swimming with the whales, dear. I'll do everything to make sure you get to do it."

Once she was able to part the gravity defying raindrops from her not-so-recent memory, Melanie was able to remember what he was talking about. He had booked an excursion with the expensive and exclusive *Amazing Sea Tours*. She had once mentioned her dream (which had started with a childhood fascination with Shamu) of swimming with whales to her husband. Ralph was as generous with his money in the way that wealthy business owners weren't, so he was happy to help her. It was the only time Mel had been happy with him.

But swimming with the whales would come later. Now it was time to get trashed.

Ralph stopped drinking after three beers or so and pathetically tried to make Melanie do the same. She needed far more than three drinks to put up with him. By the time the first raindrop had fallen, she had partaken in almost everything on the cocktail menu and made several passes at Tyler, who still remained uninterested.

"I think I'm going to head to the room to get some rest before dinner. C'mon, you should join me."

Ew. God, no. "I'll meet you there. I'm gonna grab one more drink." Her beautiful voice refused to sound slurred. That would taint her image. He tried to protest, but arguing with her was not dissimilar to asking a shark to go vegan.

As Ralph made his way to the room, Melanie made her way back to the tiki-bar. Tyler was getting ready to close in preparation for the storm.

"Hey," she greeted him in the most seductive voice she could manage in her inebriated state.

"We're closing up," Tyler warned, keeping his distance.

"That's good. That means you'll be free soon. And what will you be doing in your free time?"

"Probably calling my wife." If that was meant to be a warning to back off, Melanie didn't care.

"Screw her." Melanie reached out to try to stroke his arm. "I bet you can do better."

"Hard pass."

That put Melanie off guard. "I see. You think you'll feel guilty if you cheat on her. But I'll tell you something: there's no shame in taking what you want."

Tyler gave his best professional look of disgust. "Look, you've had way too much to drink. You need to get to bed."

Mel smirked. "You could bring me there."

Tyler face palmed before grabbing a flashing turtle cup. They were the only cups he had yet to pack away. He put some ice and water into it before handing it out to her. "Take this and get out of here before I call someone to escort you."

Melanie glared at him. She didn't like being rejected, but she also didn't need security telling Ralph about this. His damn kids try hard enough to make him suspicious of her; she didn't need someone proving them right. "Fine."

She snatched the turtle away from him and stomped inside. Stomping turned to stumbling as she made her way to the promenade. She refused numerous offers of help in the most biting tone she could muster. She was angry with the whole world. How *dare* he reject her?

She took this anger all the way to the end of the promenade until confusion took over her.

Where exactly was her cabin?

She eyed the sign at the far end wall, behind a few lounge chairs:

Floor 5: Cabins 4000-4990
Floor 4: Cabins 3000-3999
Floor 3: Promenade
Floor 2: Cabins 2000-2999
Floor 1: Casino, Theater, Club, Dining Hall

In accompaniment to this sign was a staircase tucked neatly behind the wall. She knew her phone was not on her, as she had missed the luxury of scrolling through it while her husband talked. Calling Ralph to come get her was not an option. She took a moment to try to think of a number that sounded like it could be familiar, but all she could think of was raindrops. She decided to try the second floor in an attempt to see what looked familiar.

She clutched the railing and her turtle cup as she went down the stairs. When she reached the bottom, she felt as if someone had just taken her off her eighth consecutive ride of the *Tilt-A-Whirl*. She leaned against a large windowpane that made up the right wall to catch her balance.

She looked outside to see the sky had given up raining cats and dogs and was throwing down wolves and lions instead. It looked like someone was dropping liquid sheets to the water below. The wind whipped the water under the overhang and onto the thin catwalk meant for employees outside. The waves below seemed to be in a MMA fight as they thrashed against the side of the boat. A flash of light lit up the otherwise dark sky in order to display something moving in the water.

Was that a fin?

Mel pressed her face against the glass to get a better look.

The next flash of lightning confirmed her earlier suspicions.

It must be a whale! Something in her drunken perception told her that it had to be a whale. A wave of excitement propelled her towards the emergency exit at the far end of the glass wall. She stumbled as she ran towards it. *Finally! I can swim with the whales!*

The door was hard to open against the wind and it forced shut quickly behind her. The wind sent water to greet her, soaking rain through her sundress. She didn't care. Melanie didn't care when the wind attempted to push her back onto the railing. She didn't care when the wind blew her flashing turtle into the sea below. She didn't care when she could hardly get herself up onto the railing in her sandals. A flash of lightning encouraged her forward by revealing the fin once more. Melanie quickly realized she *did* care when she hit the water. That was when the waves knocked sobriety back into her.

The waves toppled onto her. She could just barely tread water in her panicked state as her adrenaline kicked in.

She had to get back on board.

"Help! HELP!" Each time she opened her mouth to scream, more salt water got knocked into it. When she coughed, even more water went down her throat. She tried swimming for the ship, but the closer she got, the more dangerous the water became. The wake of the ship combined with the churning sea meant certain death if she were to try to conquer it.

They'll look for me in no time, she told herself. *All I have to do is stay afloat.*

Then, she had an idea: the whale. She had heard somewhere that dolphins sometimes helped drowning people. Maybe whales did the same? At least holding onto the whale would give her something stable enough until help came. She used her adrenaline to make her way through the waves, straining against the brick walls of water that threatened to send her under. Another flash of lightning told her she was getting closer. And closer. When she grabbed the fin, her face fell.

It was not a whale at all, but a floating pile of garbage. What she had in her hand was a plastic pipe with a piece of cloth clinging to it. As her last hope faded, she decided to try to climb onto the island of waste. Unfortunately for her, this was not a very sturdy pile, and it sent her below the waves.

Her eyes opened underwater despite the sting. In the blackness, she saw the flickering of the turtle's eyes as it floated safely in the water above her before the battery gave out.

There was no way she would let that stupid turtle live and not her. She forced herself to swim up. Garbage now rested in the beauty queen's blonde hair.

Her next plan of action was to follow the boat. She had to stay close if they were going to find her. She fought against the waves in an effort to keep up. She was desperate, but she was also exhausted. As she gasped for air, a wave sent more water down her throat. Another came crashing down over her, sending her under. In her panic, she took a breath, and her lungs started to burn. She was no longer swimming but struggling frantically as she tried to push herself to the surface. It was no use. Her body was not getting oxygen and it was starting to give out. As she looked skyward, a flash of lightning showed the silhouette of the turtle cup. A look down below showed the abyss.

As she started to drift towards unconsciousness, a feeling of peace came over her. Maybe this would not be so bad. It would all be over soon. That was when her feet hit something hard. Solid. Her feeling of serenity evaporated and turned to confusion. She recognized this sensation as the ground. She couldn't be at the bottom of the ocean yet. Could she? Instinctively, she looked up.

Thick raindrops poured upwards as Melanie stared into the abyss above her.

The Pains of Writing

Case No. FN2187-217-4
Date: June 10, 2021
Reporting Officer: Det. Murphy Hayworth
Prepared by: Officer Julisa Chevron
Incident: self-mutilation and suicide

Details of Event:
~~This is my first police report. They went over this in the academy, but to be honest, I skipped that day. Not because it was about police reports, I actually love to write. It was my birthday. This is incredibly off topic, perhaps I should start over.~~
On June 10th, 2021, the Honorable Judge Julius Reignheart ordered a wellness and safety check on Mr. Nathan Douglas. He neglected to turn up for his court date and he would not return the calls of his ex-wife, Nicole Douglas née Rutherford, or his children. ~~Honestly, it was very nice of the judge to even bother, as divorce court tends to go on whether both parties are there or not. Judge Reignheart had a pretty nasty divorce the other year, though, so maybe he just felt sympathetic? Who knows?~~ I was sent by dispatch to his home at 237 Eggert Ave. It was a nice bi-level home, surrounded on two sides by houses that looked exactly like it, identical copies, except painted different colors. ~~I guess that means that they aren't identical copies, but it appeared as though they were built around the same time, with some sort of theme in mind: the Eggert neighborhood model homes. The Douglas home had a basketball hoop outside, which I accidentally knocked into, sorry again about the car. It didn't seem like the Douglas family was any nicer to their stuff, I mean, their mailbox was crooked. I'm getting off track again.~~ I approached the front door and knocked. No response. There was an awful stench, like curdled milk and sweaty gym socks had a baby that was horrified of its own creation so it committed suicide. This is a dramatic description, but it is important to note, as it gave me probable cause. I knocked again to similar results. I walked to the side window, careful not to step on dying forget-me-nots. It was then that I saw Mr. Douglas, his head slumped on his laptop. On his lap was what looked like a pink, bloody cat, only it was a pile of

organs. A longer one, what seemed like one of the intestines, trailed down to the floor. The end of it curled around the wheel of his chair. A baseball bat with streaks of dark brown dried on it lay nearby. I called for backup immediately after throwing up.

Video Journal One: Are ya happy.mov

Nathan Douglas sat in a black office chair. The back was noticeably tattered, with some stuffing poking out from the seams. There was an indent through the center of it, making the sides puff outwards, giving the chair a bowl-like shape. Nathan was leaning forward, arms crossed on the top of his desk. His glasses were notably smudged, so he squinted at the monitor before him. He wasn't centered, instead shifted more to the right of the screen. Over his left shoulder was an island standing guard over the kitchen, the only separation from the living room. If he moved to his left, one would see the couch pointed at a modestly sized TV, but he was unlikely to do so, as he worked better on his right side.

"I don't think I've seen someone use a video journal since… Well, I haven't seen anyone do it in real life." Nathan pushed up his glasses by the bridge. "It seems sort of antiquated, doesn't it? They had that audio journal in *Dracula*, but even that old trope has gone to shit." He pressed his mouth into a thin line, his pale pink lips disappearing until *pop*, his mouth was back open. "But what's the point of going to therapy if I don't listen, right? I've gotta admit, I'm self-conscious looking at myself. God knows I won't play it back, I bet I sound shitty today. I had a few drinks yesterday and, yeah, I know you said that's not a good idea, but I needed one or two. Life's stressful. I don't know what I'd even say today, so I might cut it short, come back when I have something interesting for you."

Nathan moved an arm from the table and clicked a button on his laptop, ending the video.

Details of Event (cont.):

Mr. Douglas was seeing a psychiatrist in combination with therapy. His psychiatrist, Dr. Lindsay Corbin, met with her patient monthly. He was prescribed lamotrigine and fluoxetine. His therapist, Dylan Thompson, could not speak to the police about his client's sessions due to client confidentiality. ~~It seems pointless to protect what he said after he killed himself. What's he going to do,~~

<del>file a HIPAA claim? Not likely.</del> Thompson did tell us that the videos found on his laptop were part of his therapy, since he felt that talking through the logic of his thoughts and actions would be helpful for Douglas, and that it could give him someone to talk to. <del>I'll have to describe some of them here in order to display what looks like a descent into madness. I've only seen the first one so far, but I can see why Mrs. Douglas left him. He looks like a wiry weirdo. His hair was all over the place and he couldn't even look directly at the camera. What's he so nervous about?</del>

Video Journal Two: Bitchface.mov
Nathan leaned back in his chair; arms crossed over his chest. His glasses were still smudged, his brown hair still askew. "I really can't believe her audacity. I mean, what the *actual* fuck?" He reached out of the camera's view, retrieving a *Heineken*, which he proceeded to take a swig from. Instead of replacing it, he held it by the neck, using the arm of the chair as a sort of coaster. "I just got off the phone with Ben. He's got some stuff left at the house that he wants to grab. I told him I'd take him to get some food, y'know, like dads do. And *what* does he say to me?" Nathan cleared his throat dramatically, an actor preparing for his debut. "'What makes you want to spend time with me all of a sudden?' Can you believe that kid? I pressed him a bit, and he finally admitted his *mother* told him that I care more about writing than the family."

Nathan lifted the bottle to his lips, splashing a bit on his plaid shirt. He scowled, but took a gulp anyway. "Ben's sixteen years old. He's got friends, at least one girlfriend, baseball, he's practically the mayor of Sea County for God's sake! He's busy in his own right. If he asked me to do things with him, of course I'd do them."

Nathan rubbed his thumb up and down the bottle's neck, casting a glance out in the distance. He pushed his glasses up by the bridge with his left hand, bringing his bottle to his lips with his right. "I'll admit, I've been writing a lot recently. Did I miss a few games? Sure. Ben should be old enough to understand I do it for him, for the family. He's got college in two years. If my book takes off, I mean *really* takes off, he won't have to worry."

He straightened up in his chair, this time adjusting his glasses by his frames, a smile splitting his cheeks, showing the tips of stalagmites in his upper jaw. "I don't see why it *wouldn't*. My sister,

Kate, she's gonna give it a read for me when I finish. She's a big shot editor at the… Well, the name's not important, but her input's going to be a great help. She can't publish me there, y'know, 'cause she mostly deals with YA, that sort of thing. My book's definitely *adult*, but she has connections. It's gonna be a hit."

His mouth pressed into a line. "But that bitch had to turn it into something negative. Look, I know it's not healthy to be badmouthing the mother of your kids, but she's turning them against me! The hell am I supposed to do, shake her hand?" He let out a breath that crackled with the hint of a whistle, though it didn't last long enough to hit a note. "What she doesn't understand is that writing takes time. I can't just sit down and secrete a novel out of my ass. It takes time. Especially this one. I'm going for the fantasy-horror genre and that requires a lot of world building. I won't bore you with the details, but the piece takes place in a medieval-esque time period and I want to have all my books on the shelf. Is that a good metaphor? Maybe I should write that down."

Nathan leaned forward, placing his beer bottle back out of sight. The screen showed only the plaid of his shirt until he reappeared with a pocket notebook in his left hand, scribbling away with his right. "Not the best metaphor, I guess, but you can never be too careful. Sometimes I come up with a real zinger, but I'll forget it if I don't write it down. What was I talking about before?"

His fingers tapped against the arm of his chair in a wave. "Oh yeah, research. I don't see the point in writing if you can't express truth through the page. Not some philosophical bullshit version of truth either, I'm talking reality on the page. Art imitates reality, I forget who said it, but the sentiment holds. There's no point in writing if you can't immerse your reader in the reality you build up and let's face it, it's much easier to do it if you stay as close to reality as possible. It limits how much disbelief you need to get the reader to suspend. I want this to be as real as possible, and you can only do that with the truth. *That's* why I research so much, that's why I miss out on some of Ben's games, or Molly's recitals, or whatever the fuck I've missed since I've started this book. Probably a lot, maybe too much, but I'll make it up to them when I hit it big. They might side with their mom now, but who're they going to side with when they need tuition?"

Details of Event (cont.):

Mr. Douglas starts off pretty normal in the beginning. Maybe he's a bit bitter, maybe he's a bit too cocky about his writing, but he doesn't seem the type to somersault off the precipice, at least not yet. Who knows if the stuff even holds up? Mr. Douglas isn't published, at least not yet, but that doesn't mean much. ~~I mean, I'm not published. I've been writing since high school and I really enjoy it. My dad told me that people who write make no money and blow their brains out more often than not. I like myself, and I like others, so I became a cop instead. You'd be surprised how many interesting characters you meet out on patrol, as well as in office. I've only been at Sea County a month or two, but I have enough to write five novels. This isn't about me though. I should probably get back to watching these videos.~~

Video Journal Five: Tired.mov

Nathan holds two transparent orange bottles in his hands between his thumb and forefinger. He holds them both out in front of him, labels facing away from the camera. "These things are spawns of Satan's hatred for humanity. They're supposed to help me, but this *one*..." He moves a bottle close to the camera. "Makes me dizzy. And *this* one..." He tosses the former over his shoulder, which hits the floor with a *clack, thump* as it rolls against the wall off camera. The next medication approaches the camera now. "This one keeps me up all night. I can't even write, because I feel exhausted, but when I lay down, I just... Lie there. It's hell."

Nathan sighed, pushing his glasses up the bridge. His fingers stood on the chair's arm like a spider, his nails digging into the cushion. "I can't show this one to you, or you'll make me take it. Maybe I'll show you this if I can get Dr. Corbin to change my meds, so you can see the mentality I was forced into. I don't know. I'll decide later."

Autopsy Report

Decedent: Nathan Douglas
Age: 47
DOB: 10/27/1974
Sex: M

Case No. FN2187-217-4
Means: suicide
ID By: At scene
Autopsy: Todd Tony, MD

Findings:

Fluoxetine levels low, suggesting that it was not taken for around a month.

Lamotrigine levels at zero, suggesting that it was not taken for around a month.

Video Journal Fourteen: Fuckukate.mov

Nathan's face was red. His hair stood just like it shouldn't be able to in earth's gravity. His left hand was in his hair, squeezed into a fist, brown hair poking through his fingers like weeds in a sidewalk. His glasses were now clean, yet slightly fogged. His cheeks were wet, trails of tears visible like rain on a window. "She didn't like it."

Silence overpowered sniffs as he reached behind the computer for a *Heineken.* "I really don't get it. Do you know what she said about it? It's *too vague* and *too expository.* She doesn't want details thrown at her. How else is the audience supposed to know that I did research? Are they supposed to *guess?*" He took a swig from the bottle. "I did *so much* research. I thought I was so close to the truth, but apparently not. My descriptions are too dry, she said. Dry, vague, expository. Don't these all sound like opposites? How can it be vague if I'm using 'too much exposition?' How can it be dry if I have all those *details*? Maybe she doesn't know how to make up her fucking mind."

Nathan put down the bottle off camera, before putting both his elbows on his desk and his head in his hands. "She has to like it. If my own sister doesn't like it, how is it going to be big? How am I going to make it up to Ben and Molly then? I need to pay for their college or else... or else..." His fingers stretched under his glasses, covering his eyes. His shoulders fell up and down, over and over, with low whines akin to a malfunctioning microwave. "I have to make it up to them, I have to. Or else I'm going to lose them. I can't lose them, I can't let them hate me. I just have to work harder. If I work harder, I'll be able to do it."

Details of Event (cont.):

Mr. Douglas seemed to fall into a desperate state. Poor guy, I feel for him. He just wanted to see his kids, and to make them like him. Maybe if he worked on being there for them *now* rather than in their future, they'd appreciate him more. ~~This is probably stuff his therapist should have told him. Maybe he did, but since Mr. Douglas is getting worse and worse on camera, he's either not listening, or his therapist wasn't very good.~~ One thing is for sure, he really took to these video messages. Although Mr. Thompson knew that Mr. Douglas was making these videos, he seemed surprised by the number of them. There were a lot, around fifty or so made in a month. Some are five minutes, some are ten. ~~That's why it's taking me so long to review them. I know you all want your report in sooner, but there's a lot to go through. This isn't exactly my idea of a Netflix binge.~~ The videos become more and more about writing, until, suddenly, it's his suicide. Poor guy. Poor kids. Poor family. I hope that, one day, they can find solace in everything.

-Officer Julisa Chevron

Nathan Douglas' Phone Records

User:

Hey, Kate, get a chance to read the newest draft?

Kate:

Going to finish it up tonight, I got sidetracked.

User:

Get serious, Kate.

User:

This is important. Ben needs to go to college.

Kate:

Nate, I don't want you to get your hopes up.

Kate:
Only like 1% of authors make that kind of money.

User:
So now you don't believe in me?

Kate:
I didn't say that.

User:
I can read between the lines.

Kate:
Nate, you always do this. You thrust yourself into these huge ideas, you put all your energy into them, never finish, OR you get all wounded when things don't work out.

Kate:
You can't just wake up one day and say you want to write a book.

User:
How dare you?
User:
I've been writing since kindergarten.
You of all people should know that.
Just because I chose to work
in the real world before writing
my book doesn't make me less of a writer.
User:
You know what? Forget this. I'll do
this on my own.
User:
I don't need you. Who the fuck
knows your company anyways?
You'll be sorry when you see me
in the fucking Penguin publishing
company. Whatever it's called.

Kate:
Yeah, okay, good luck with that(:

Video Journal 20: Newplan.mov

"I've decided that I'm going to start using this more." Nathan is wearing a stained, oversized T-shirt. "I was thinking about it and this is way better than my notebook, y'know? Much more real. When I have an idea, I can record it here, that way I can hear the emotion that comes along with the idea, what words I need to stress, that kind of thing." He adjusts his glasses by his frames. A wiry smile spreads across his face. There is soft drumming as his fingers *tap tap* against the chair's arm.

"Don't you think that is closer to truth? Not the truth, truth with a capital 'T,' the epistemic truth. This story is going to be renowned, sensational, because it is going to be the realest, most truthful piece of fiction there is. I've done so much research. I can't show you my notes, because they're on the laptop, but I've read a lot of medical journals. Kate said some stuff was vague, and she's right, there was some vagueness all around the horror. Maybe it's just because I'm not used to writing it. I've always liked fantasy more, but thrillers are what sells. Thrillers are kind of brutal, right?"

His shoulders rise up to his ears. "If they aren't, then fuck it. My fantasy-horror-thriller will have plenty of violence. I just need to figure out how to write it."

Nathan Douglas' Phone Records

The Bitch:
Hey

User:
God damn it what do you want

The Bitch:
Daddy its Molly

User:
Sorry baby!! I thought you were someone else.

The Bitch:
Cause u hate mom now

User:
I don't hate your mom. Adults just grow apart sometimes.

The Bitch:
OK daddy

User:
Did your mom tell you to text me?

The Bitch:
She wants to know if ur coming to graduation

User:
Who's graduating?

The Bitch:
me from fifth grade u said ud try to come remember?
The Bitch:
can u not come

User:
When is it again?

The Bitch:
saturday

User:
I'll be there. I love you, baby girl.

The Bitch:
i luv u 2 daddy

Video Journal Forty-One: Writingishard.mov

"Sometimes writing makes me want to drive a nail through my foot. That way, I can martyr myself for artists everywhere like Jesus fucking Christ himself." Nathan's hand was pressed against his forehead with his elbow resting just before his laptop. His eyes squeezed shut for a while, before opening. "I'm trying so hard. There's so much shit I need to get fixed in this piece, but I can only do so much. I didn't go to medical school. How am I supposed to know how a crushed foot looks? Or how much pain someone'll be in when they're finger's cut off? Do all writers sit in the back of a hospital to make their gore look realistic? Sound realistic? Should I do the same?" His hand moved down his face to the bridge of his nose. "I'll figure something out. I just have to put my mind to it is all. If I think really hard, I'll pull it off. Right?"

Nathan Douglas' Phone Records

The Bitch:
I really hope your happy. Your daughter was looking forward to seeing you at her graduation. You promised her you would try to show up. I saw the texts myself. And you don't fucking show up. Worse than that, you couldn't even bother to call her? What the fuck is wrong with You??? You tell me you love your kids and want what's best for them but you pull this shit? Clearly you don't care. You better PRAY the kids want to see you. PRAY. I won't keep you away from them, but your gonna have to fight your ass off to see them in court. You've never shown any interest in your own fucking kids. Maybe you should start trying.

Video Journal Forty-Nine: How.mov

"I can't focus on writing anymore. How could I? She's going to try to keep my kids. How could she do this to me?" There are no tears now, but Nathan's voice drips with the prospect of them. "I write all the time for *them*. Everything I do is for *them*. Does that make me a bad father? Will I still be a bad father, even if I pay off their debts? No. No, I won't be. I'll have more time to spend with them, once the book's published, once I don't have to work on it anymore. Then they'll be set for life. We'll all be set for life together."

Nathan is slumped back in his chair. His head is just barely shown on screen, appearing over his desk like the sun sinking beyond the horizon. "What am I supposed to do? How am I supposed to win them over? Win them back from that bitch? I'm sure she tells them awful things about me, their own dad. How could they believe her? They're old enough to draw their own conclusions, aren't they?"

Nathan reached out and took his bottle of *Heineken* from the desk. He took a long drink, draining its contents, before slamming the bottle against the floor. The shattered glass could be seen in the living room behind him, splattered like thrown paint. It was then that he sat up.

"I just need to make this realistic. I just have to add truth to this piece. But how? How do I make these descriptions better? It's not like I can transport back to medieval times, watch my characters hurt themselves, and…"

Nathan stood, his chair flying backwards. The wheels hitting the glass sounded like nails on the sidewalk. "I have an idea."

Video Journal Fifty:
WIN_FN21872174_1027_30_06_21

Nathan was not on camera. The computer was pushed back far enough so that the couch was now visible. *Slam*. A door closed. *Thump*. A cabinet closed as well. "The first big gory scene is the robbery one. You see, this guy tries to steal from the king, so he gets his fingers cut off one by one."

Nathan came back into frame with a bag of carrots, a *Dalstrong* knife, and a grin. He's in the center of the frame. "They say experience is the best teacher, don't they?" He slipped a carrot from the bag, waving it in front of the camera, before placing his left hand down on the desk. "I used to make this dish, usually on Thanksgiving. It was a side dish, nothing special. Honey glazed carrots. They used to be Ben's favorite. Molly likes them better raw."

Nathan lifted the knife. "They say that fingers have the same thickness as carrots. If I just... Start with the carrots..." The knife moved up and down across the desk, moving toward the rest. *Thump, thump, thump.* As he got further down, his knife began to hesitate longer with each cut. Until *thUNK.* The knife came back up stained red. He lifted his hand, inspecting it before the camera. His ring finger was missing. Blood trickled down his palm and sprouted upwards, a geyser erupting. "Oh God... Oh fuck. Okay. Okayokayokay. Fuck fuck. I should... I can wrap the towel around it to stop it while I describe this. Okayokay." He held his wrist away from his body, his right hand a vice around it. "It didn't hurt as bad as I thought it would. Maybe I'm in shock. What does shock feel like? This feels like... I'm watching myself from afar. I don't want to think too much about the blood. Oh God there's so much." As he spoke, he retreated from the camera, towards the kitchen. He reached for a towel, a yellow one with watermelons, which he pressed to his fingers. The red immediately started to infect the towel.

"I still have to do another one, don't I? What do I still have? Oh, fuck, I do, I do." Nathan looked down at his hand, his chin pressed against his chest. The yellow disappeared, the blood was dripping onto the carpet below. "I'm not going to be able to write about this and get back into it. I have to keep going. I'll keep going, get some writing done, and then... Is it illegal to do this shit to yourself? It's got to be. They're gonna think that I'm too crazy for my kids... Oh God, oh fuck. Focus, okay. The next things... The foot. A peasant's foot is crushed by a horse. I... Don't have one of those. What can I do instead?"

He paced back and forth, cradling his arm like a newborn. "Okay, you know what? I just need something I can use to put pressure on it. Like... ah..." He pushed his glasses up by the bridge, before snapping. "Got it. I'll be right back."

Nathan left the camera rolling as he left the frame. There was soft padding up and down the stairs before he returned. In his hand, he held a metal baseball bat. "Ben meant to come pick this up. Who knows! Maybe his mother bought him some new equipment by now." He held the bat horizontally, right beside his waist. "I'm thinking the best way to do this is to just... put the flat part against my foot and... push. That should work, right? I don't weigh as much as a horse, but it's the same principle. At least, it should be."

He looked down at his feet, and his thumb started to move up and down the bat's cushioned grip. He positioned it on his foot once, twice, before deciding on a spot. His left hand rested atop his right. Blood trickled down the bat from the overused towel. "Okay... I can do this... This is for my kids. This is for their future. I can do this." He started to exert pressure on his foot, but he didn't seem too troubled. It was when he leaned down on top of it that the tears intermingled with blood, clearing some of the splatters from his cheeks. The bat itself began to shake, though he remained persistent with the pressure. A sound like crinkled shopping bags and broken *Lays* chips dominated the air. After a while, Nathan collapsed forward, his right hand gripping the back of his chair. This proved not to be enough support, however, as he promptly collapsed to the ground. His hair, a withered brown grass, could be seen at the bottom right of the screen.

"Oh, God... It hurts too much. Oh my God oh my fuck, why did I do that? I have to stop this I... How the fuck am I going to write about this? There's no way... I feel... I can't think straight. How am I supposed to write? Oh God... Ben, Molly, you're not getting this book. I've wasted... for so long... How can I ever make it up to you? I'm sorry, I'm sorry, I'm..."

Nathan suddenly popped up at the bottom of the screen, like a meerkat from their underground home. Tears and blood pooled on his face, on his glasses, but his lips pressed together. His vision was cast to something off screen. The handle of the bat came in the frame as he used it for leverage to get up and crawl into his chair.

"If I can only do one more thing for my kids, it should be a good one. Not a disappointment." He grabbed something from off screen, bringing the butcher knife into view. Shards of glass were embedded in his hands. "Artists are worth a lot more dead, aren't they?" A tear slipped down his cheek. "I love you kids." Nathan jammed the knife into his stomach, pulling it across in a jagged line. Before a scream could register on his lips, his head fell against the keyboard with a gurgle.

Sea County Insurance
Owner and Beneficiary Information
Owner: Nathan Douglas
Beneficiary: Ben and Molly Douglas.
Life Insurance Benefit Information
Amount of Insurance: $1,000,000
<u>Denied by reason of suicide</u>

Kali

Doctor Lynne Carr's heels clicked against the speckled tile floors as she walked briskly down the hallway. The stark white walls gave her a headache that she aimed to cure with her *Starbucks* ice blonde caffè americano. Awaiting her down the hall were Detectives John Carmen and Katelyn Guillermo. They sipped their own, likely stale, coffee from ceramic mugs as they peered through the one-way mirror. The detectives didn't look her way until Lynne was practically standing on top of them.

"I presume Kali is in there waiting for me?" Dr. Carr punctuated her question with a sip of her beverage.

It was Guillermo that answered her first. "Listen, Lynne, it might be better if one of us-"

"You'll only intimidate her, Kate," Carr warned. "You can come in if things escalate, but not before."

Guillermo looked to Carmen, who only gave a solemn nod of approval in response.

Kate sighed. "Fine. Just be careful, okay?"

"I don't think you'll need to worry." Carr maneuvered past the detectives to enter the interrogation room. The usual barren landscape had been changed to provide comfort to the witness. There were sheets of printer paper with assorted Sharpies and highlighters on the table for Kali to use. Several of these papers had scribbles on them, with the artist's signature printed proudly on them. It read *"KaL i."* The lowercase A's had a tendency to look like a lowercase P, and the Ls were backwards.

Kali did not sit by the table anymore. She opted to play with a Raggedy Anne doll on the floor. This doll was often used for children to display where they had been touched in court cases but served now as an excellent playmate. Raggedy Anne had her feet dragged across the floor to imitate walking. Kali hummed "The Wheels on the Bus" as the doll walked on to an unknown destination.

"Can I play with you?" Dr. Carr offered.

Kali looked up from her doll, only to turn her attention to the floor. "I don't have another toy for you."

"That's okay. I don't mind just talking with her."

Kali considered this, before nodding her head over and over. She scooted on the floor into the corner to make room for her new playmate. Doctor Carr placed her cup of coffee on the stainless-steel table before she took a seat on the floor next to her.

"Hi, Raggedy Anne, I'm-"

"That's not her name," Kali interrupted. "It's Mary."

"Sorry, Mary. I'm Doctor Lynne."

This made Kali squirm. She curled her short brown hair around her finger. "Are you mad at me?"

Lynne furrowed her brow. "Why would I be mad at you?"

" 'Cause I saw Doctor Michael get real hurt, and I didn't do nothing to help him."

"No, sweetie," she said. "That wasn't your fault. There was nothing you could have done."

Kali didn't respond. Instead, she drew her knees up to her chest and rested her forehead on them. Lynne eyed her for a moment as she carefully picked out what she wanted to say to her.

"You know, Kali, there is a way you can help."

Kali responded with silence.

"You can tell me what happened, and I can try to make this right. Not just for you, but for your friends."

"Liam is *not* my friend," Kali whimpered. "He's mean."

"Well, if you tell me the truth, we can see about never letting Liam near you again. Would you like that?"

Kali's forehead moved up and down against her knee.

"Alright then, Kali, start from the beginning."

***

Doctor Michael had a lot of cool things to play with. A play-kitchen, a tub full of sand, and loads of board games. Today, they sat at a table coloring some pictures. The doctor was too big for both his chair and the table, so his knees were stuck against its side as he sat. A toy phone sat between his shoulder and ear. Kali's toy phone was in her free hand. She used her other hand to scribble on the paper. Her tongue stuck out as she concentrated.

Adam and Liam stood against the far wall, by the shelves that held all of the games. Kali had left them there when she came to the session.

"So, Kali," the doctor began, "How long have you known Adam?"

It was Adam, not Kali, who answered the question. "Since she was born."

Michael looked at Adam with surprise. "I had no idea you would be joining us this session, Adam."

Kali looked back at Adam and his friend.

"What do you mean, Doc?" Adam raised a brow. "We've been here the whole time."

"He's just an asshole, Adam," Liam growled. "He only ever talks to one of us at a time. Ain't that right?"

Liam had only recently started coming to sessions. As the conversation material got more serious, Adam seemed to need him around. Kali wasn't a big fan of Liam, since he got angry really fast. She was smart enough to know she shouldn't talk when he did. Adam had taught her to respect his friend, regardless of whether or not she liked him. He thought that Liam could help the two of them. Kali wasn't so sure.

"I'm sorry," the doctor responded. "Why don't you join us?"

Adam looked to Liam, who was busy glaring at the psychiatrist. Adam shrugged and moved to sit crisscross-applesauce beside the table. Liam loomed over him.

"Now, Adam," Dr. Michael began as he slid his glasses back up his nose. "You knew Kali since birth?"

"Yes, I was there when she was born." As Adam nodded, his short yet shaggy brown hair moved into his eyes. He moved it back to the side, before casting a soft smile to Kali. She returned it and toyed with a strand of her hair.

"Is that so?"

"Well, she is my sister. Why wouldn't I be?" Adam cocked his head to the side as the doctor wrote something down on the construction paper before him.

"Shouldn't you know this already?" Liam blurted out. "For fuck's sake, do you even *read* your patient's files?"

Dr. Michael looked at Adam with a weary smile. "Sorry, but I always like to confirm these things."

"It's alright, Doc," Adam assured him. "I really don't mind."

Liam went silent.

"Now, Adam, you and Kali just moved out of your parents' house. Is that correct?"

"Yes, I take care of her now," Adam confirmed. As Michael wrote something down, Adam craned his neck to see. The doctor's scrawl was illegible to Adam.

Liam could make it out.

"Why is it that you moved, Adam?" Dr. Michael eyed the man as he squirmed in his spot.

"I just did. I'm twenty-four, I have a decent job, it just seemed… like a good time, you know?"

Dr. Michael nodded. "Why is it that Kali moved with you?"

" 'Cause I wanted her to."

"Just because *you* wanted her to? What did your parents say?"

"My dad was fine with it."

"And your mom? Surely, she didn't want her six-year-old daughter taken away?"

Adam stared hard at the psychiatrist for a moment. "Mother didn't have a say. It was the best thing for Kali, even Dad agreed."

"Why's that, Adam?"

Kali began to cry. Adam wiped a tear off of his own cheek. He seemed to sink into his seat on the floor. "Just 'cause."

"That's not a great reason to take someone's child from their home."

"Why the fuck do you have to pester him? You know the reason! Is this how you get off? Watching a little girl and a grown man cry as you bring up shit you already know too fucking well? Huh? Is that your game, you sick little fuck? It's not fucking funny. You're being a sick asshole, just like *she* was." Liam snapped. He suddenly pounced forward and slammed his hands against the table.

Kali jumped back, knocking her chair over in the process.

Adam stayed still.

Dr. Michael stood his ground, remaining in his seat, but his knuckles went white around his pen.

Liam snarled.

"It's important for them to process this if they want to grow past it, Liam," the doctor tried.

"He doesn't have *jack shit* to live past. I'm the one that beat her. That bitch deserved it!"

"Why did she-"

"Do you know *nothing*? She beat Adam and his Pop senseless. When she wasn't doing that, she would scream at them till the neighbors called the cops. That bitch had them so fucking scared that they wouldn't dream of telling the cops the truth. They had to lie through their teeth, say, 'Mommy Dearest is perfect. It was our fault' so that she could live to beat them another day. Adam just knew it wouldn't be long until she beat Kali, so he ran off with her. But that *bitch*. She couldn't leave well enough alone. So, when she appeared at their apartment, I had to stop her. My only regret is that the bitch didn't die."

Dr. Michael stared at him for a while. "Adam…"

"Adam doesn't want to talk to you now. You made his fucking sister cry. No, you're going to talk to *me*. I'm sick and tired of you ignoring me, like I'm some fucking disease. That's what you think I am, right? A fucking disease? Some symptom that Adam can ignore and sleep off? You're dead fucking wrong. I'm here, and you are going to talk to me."

"Liam, please, I would really like to talk with Adam just to-"

It was then that Liam flipped the table. Construction paper and crayons scattered across the floor. Liam charged forward, knocking Dr. Michael back to the floor. He debated leaning down to strangle the doctor with his tie, but he had a better idea — one that would teach him a much better lesson. The small pink chair Kali once sat on lay by Dr. Michael's legs. Liam picked up the chair, and stood over the doctor.

Kali cowered off in the corner with her brother.

"You never listen to me. I'm fucking sick of you!" Liam raised the chair over his mop of brown hair before he slammed the chair down on the psychiatrist. He did this over and over as Kali screamed in the background. Adam remained silent.

***

"And he hit him again and again and again and again. I screamed so loud, I wanted him to stop. But he…" Kali broke down in tears.

Lynne sat in silence. Kali's head stayed stationary, leaning against her knees as she gripped Mary the doll for comfort. She sniffled, whined, and cried, her knuckles going white.

"Hey, Kali," Carr began. "Do you want me to get you some water? It will make you feel better."

Kali nodded her head. As she did, her brown locks pushed up against her knees.

"Okay, I'll be right back, hun." The doctor pushed off the ground to stand up, and grabbed her *Starbucks* cup from the table. By now, most of the ice had melted. A reminder of how cold it once was remained in the watery scar left upon the desk. As she exited the room, she took a sip of her watered-down coffee, which did nothing to help her headache.

Guillermo and Carmen locked eyes with Carr the moment she closed the door behind her. "What's your opinion?"

"There is no way he'll be able to stand trial," Carr replied, then took another sip of her drink. "He's far too unstable. It seems that Liam comes out when Adam feels uncomfortable. If Michael could get him that upset, then a prosecutor would have him out in two seconds."

"What about Kali?" Carmen looked to the huddled mass in the corner as he asked, bringing his mug to his lips.

"I think she's a coping mechanism," Carr explained. "The scared little kid gives him something to hold on to."

Lynne turned to stand before the one-way mirror. In the corner sat Adam. Only his shaggy brown hair was visible, as his face was buried in Mary the doll. His shoulders rose and fell with his high-pitched sobs that they could faintly hear from behind the glass.

The Cult

This story is written in the style and universe of H.P. Lovecraft. I hope you enjoy it, regardless of whether my own style is missing!

It is both gnawing guilt and unceasing thoughts that move my hands to write. Guilt is unfounded, some may say, if what you perceive to have done has never occurred, at least, if it has never occurred in the perception of those around you. You may think I have gone mad. I cannot argue against this myself, as of my guilt I have no proof. Yet, I *know* that what happened was not some illusion of my senses. I *know* that the object of my guilt is not one of pure imagination. I am writing here, on this unbiased piece of paper, to impress my thoughts onto something that cannot resist or question them.

It was a cool fall day when this madness began, one that would become one of the last perfectly sane days of my life. I stood before the class in the rustic lecture hall of Miskatonic University, leaning against my desk as I spoke of times long since past. The room, as one could see, was old and yet had not fallen into disrepair. Wooden desks of exceptional quality stood before the rows of seats. The chairs themselves were cushioned and lined with leather, upheld by solid wooden legs. Some students had carved words or obscene pictures into the arms of the chairs, though the university had taken excessive care to buff out the especially grotesque.

The walls were of wooden paneling covering the bricks that made up the building and boasted ornately carved trim. The paneling, I presume, was deemed far more aesthetically pleasing than the brick alone. The floor under the students' desks was lined with the finest tiling, which was a modern addition. The tile was dark, to play off of the lighter paneling on the walls. On the windows were velvet red curtains, which were drawn so that the students could see the projection behind me without a glare. A *PowerPoint* was projected on a newly installed whiteboard, which was slowly starting to replace all of the blackboards in the building.

I was lecturing on the Salem witch trials. As they occurred in the same state as that of our university, students tended to find this lecture rather interesting. The silly game of schoolgirls had truly caused horrible consequences for many in Salem. A student towards the front of the room, Peter, asked the accursed question that triggered it all. He asked if Arkham's residents had any symptoms of the craze that overtook those in Salem, as our town had occasional whispers of veins of the occult running through it. It had been this way for centuries, though no one truly gave these stories merit. Well, that is to say no one of what the public may consider *respectable status* did. People appear every now and again claiming to have seen such and such paranormal event, or so and so daemonic cult. It was a fair question that seemed to arouse interest from the class. The short answer to his question was yes, but unfortunately, we were running out of time for the day. I informed him of a seemingly harmless book that spoke of a local occultist group that was pursued in this time period. I was such a fool! No one gave these occultists much merit, though they had claimed to be capable of monstrous feats. They were largely wiped out as paranoia of witches grew rampant, though many believe that some had escaped persecution. I foolishly did not pay this much regard. This seemed to pique interest and there was a soft murmur between several students to check out this book, but the rest of the remaining time we had went by peacefully thereafter.

The next class, two days later, I entered the room to see a majority of the students surrounding Peter as he read from a book. He told of the capturing of the head of the local occult and his subsequent hanging. I humored him by engaging in the text momentarily with the class, before drawing everyone's attention back to the lecture for the day. Scenes such as the one I had walked into that day occurred frequently, until eventually their minds seemed to belong to nothing else. They would not pay attention to lectures as they had before. They had been such an engaging class, but they now ceased to participate. They seemed to be enraptured by this particular topic. I contributed to their conversations less and less as it became more frequent. I had grown tired of hearing nothing but of this cult from them, so I offered the students a solution. I would give a special lecture on the topic of the cult they had become enthralled by at the end of the week, if they promised to pay attention to the other lectures. This resounded in a boisterous applause and an excitement that was expressed at almost obscene levels. They were the perfect models of students for the rest of that week. I reserved a room for the promised lecture, and utilized my free time to prepare the damnable speech for my students.

What I found in my research was revolting, but I could see how my students managed to grow such a fascination. The vast majority of people tend to enjoy learning of the horrifically strange aspects of life. Life, as they say, is stranger than fiction. The name of this cult was shrouded behind layers of rumor. The members of the cult themselves dared not to speak it, as it was deemed too sacred for mortal ears. The sane of those who learned of the name found it too grotesque a word to sully their mouths with. The mere citing of it could send chills down a person's spine and have a cold sweat run down their necks. Only the accursed *Necronomicon* dares to have the cult's name transcribed within its pages, but I will not write it here. The rituals of this cult, which are clearly listed in that forsaken grimoire, were almost as unspeakable as their names.

The roots of the cult, as I have found through studying various academic articles, seem to be European, although I cannot place a country of origin as it was practiced widely, and was brought to America along with some of its foremost immigrants. It was thought to have died out, aside from the few members who supposedly live in secret immortality. The arcane group gained approval, or so they claim, from an unknown and daemonic god through the screams of their victims as they were tortured. Then, once satisfied with the screams, they were to drain their victim of blood while keeping them alive for as long as possible. As they share in the forbidden nectar of their offering, the monstrous entity rewards them with rejuvenated souls that allow its followers to remain immortal. They must perform this ritual often to maintain the favor of the accursed center of their religion. Any creature will do, animal or human. They have been repulsively quoted as saying, "the younger the blood, the stronger the spirit." The cult was stopped in their disturbing actions by the peasants, who mistook them for witches in their detestable actions. Some escaped, evidently, and it is said that these people still live today and practice their forbidden and horrific rituals in secret.

I gave the students this information in my lecture. Instead of growing disgusted at the rituals that had filled me with unpleasant thoughts and a feeling of excessive distaste, they seemed to hang on my every word. Hearing about these deplorable actions seemed to fill them with the utmost satisfaction and put a twinkle in their eyes that sent shivers down my spine. The more I spoke on the topic, the more uneasy I became as I started to notice the increasing joy the students seemed to have from a lecture on a dismal topic. As I finished, I asked the class if they had any questions. With little hesitation, Peter's hand shot into the air with an unsettling eagerness.

"Are these rituals in *The Necronomicon*?"

I hesitated with my answer, as I feared where Peter may be going with this. Of all the students, he seemed the most enamored with my lecture. "I'm not sure."

Peter gave me a look, then smirked to himself. The look he gave was beyond explanation, as it was full of an evil I dare not describe. Some horrendous and malicious idea was hiding beyond that smile. As the class started to leave, I assured myself that Peter, or no one else in the class, had access to *The Necronomicon*. It was not an easy book to obtain, especially for a college student with little resources. I nearly had a moment of peace in this assurance, until I had a realization that made my heart skip a beat: *The Necronomicon* was in the university library. *He knew.*

I called the librarian on staff shortly thereafter to see that he made sure Peter did not go near the book. He was confused with my request, but he informed me someone already had checked it out, though university and library policy prevented him from telling me who. He was able to assure me, however, that it was not Peter. This washed away my anxieties in a wave of relief. I thanked him, before I retired to my office.

The research I had to complete for this lecture made me behind on papers I needed to grade and emails I needed to send. I was relieved to finally be able to begin the work I had missed. I sat down in my comfortable swivel chair, which had a gray wool cushion, with a black plastic arms and base. It was cheaper than the chairs in my lecture hall, but still durable and comfortable. My office was stacked with books and papers in an organized chaos that only I knew how to navigate. On my desk, I had pictures of my nieces, my sister and I at her wedding, and my dog, Sammy. My laptop occupied the only clean spot on my wooden desk. I opened it shortly after sitting before it.

I gazed out the window at the setting sun that overlooked a grassy area where the students would often play Frisbee, relax with a good book, or pass leisurely hours away chatting with friends on the surrounding benches. The patch of grass was surrounded by large trees that cast a shadow over the area with the setting sun. There were scarcely any students there, as it was a Friday evening. They were presumably all out with friends and living their lives. As I typed away on my laptop, dusk gave way to night. Around that time I had switched to grading papers, red pen marking here and there in order to make the proper corrections. I often get carried away with these things and was rooted in my office for quite some time. Just as I pulled out the last paper to grade, I heard a gut-wrenching shriek. This shriek made my blood drop to match the temperature to the icy pits of hell. I rushed to the windows to see what was going on, but I could not discern anything. Although the field below was black as obsidian, I could tell that the continuing shrieks came from there.

I raced from my office without another thought to try to decipher the source of this cry. I kept telling myself my imagination was acting up due to the lecture from earlier today. As I reached the bottom of the stairs, the motion sensor lights flashed on. The powerful beams illuminated the barren concrete about me, along with a few feet of the field. That is when I saw them. Figures robed in black were bent over a cat, which was the source of the unholy shrieking. I could not see under their hoods, but I saw the glimmer of a knife in one of their hands and the panicked eyes of the cat below. There were at least twenty of the figures, but only three of them were willing to get their hands dirty. One held the cat down while the other towered over it. The third was holding a book I could not currently see the contents of, but the ominous presence allowed me to assume it was *The Necronomicon*. All of the figures were looking at me now. I stood frozen in my spot for but a moment before racing forward. I do not know what I was thinking. Perhaps I thought that if I caught just one of them… But they raced away as soon as I drew near. I found myself stopped by the cat instead, inspecting her. They had broken one of the poor creature's legs. As I moved to pick her up, the cat bit me in fear. With gentle and reassuring strokes, I managed to gain her trust. She eventually let me pick her up, even as she mewled in pain.

I took the poor thing to an emergency veterinary center, where they fixed up her leg. I called the police as the doctor took care of her. They assured me that they would be on the lookout for any suspicious characters that night. The cat made it through the procedure just fine. She had to have her leg in a cast, but she would heal. As the cat did not have any collar and I had no idea how to find her owner, I brought her home and resolved to put up posters for her on Monday. Isis, as I decided to call her, curled up on my lap almost anywhere I sat down. She would nuzzle her head against me and purr loudly. She was a tabby and a truly sweet one. In the beginning, Sammy would eye the cat curiously, but he stayed away. They ended up getting along just fine by the end of the night. Isis slept by my pillow and Sammy slept at my feet without disturbing one another. My night was plagued by nightmares in which the terrified screams of Isis replayed over and over. It was the first of my never-ending nightmares.

The next day went on without incident. I was happy to get the thoughts of yesterday out of my head. I visited my sister and told her what had come to pass. She helped to calm my nerves but what helped the most was perhaps teatime with my nieces.

Things went downhill once I returned home that night. I got home late, as traffic from my sister's home had been a nightmare in and of itself. I was anxious to get to bed, and Sammy and Isis were anxious to accompany me. Sleep came easily, but I was awoken before I could begin to dream by Sammy's barking. It was a violent bark, one that I had never heard from him before. The golden retriever snarled and howled at the window. His fur was standing on its ends as he stood on the bed, ready to lunge. Isis meowed helplessly and pawed at me. Her ears were pushed back, and her fur was also standing on its ends. Something was wrong. I stood from my bed and walked cautiously to the window. I opened the curtains to look outside.

I live in the thick woods on the outskirts of Arkham, where light can barely pass between the trees from the moon. Standing just before these woods were the black robed figures. Multiple of them carried torches and they all chanted something ominous and low that I could not make out from inside. What terrified me the most was what they had done to my lawn. In the light of their torches, I could see they had sprinkled blood all over it. I could also see the source of where it came from. There were ten severed heads of animals on pikes in my yard: cat heads. I beheld them in horror, unable to look away. Evidently, one of the robed figures noticed me in the window, as they advanced to the house. They did not hold a flame, so I could not see under their hood. They took one of the pikes from the ground and raised it higher for me to better see. It was at that point I reeled away from the window and stumbled back to my bed. I trembled, hoping that they would go away, that they would do *something* other than stand menacingly still. I grabbed my phone from my nightstand and called the police, at which point the band of hooded figures dispersed, leaving the gruesome display in my yard. Although the police assured me they would guard the house, sleep would not come to me. Every time I closed my eyes I saw the heads of the animals on pikes and heard the chanting of the figures that cut through the wailing of the severed heads.

Sunday night I stayed at my sister's house, taking Sammy and Isis with me. She once again tried to soothe my anxieties, but this time she was unsuccessful. My hands trembled throughout the entire day, and I could not get a wink of sleep that night.

I had my lecture at around ten in the morning the next day. I was sleep deprived and looked that way. I did not hear the usual chattering when I walked in. Silence. When I came into view, I noticed something that made me tremble. They were all staring at me. Not the normal engaged or expectant stare students had, but an empty and cold stare, matched with blank expressions. I asked them how their weekends went. I received no response. I asked them how they enjoyed the lecture they had been dying for. Peter smirked that evil grin matched with dead eyes. He did not say anything more. I felt as though running from the room was the proper thing to do.

I gave about half my intended lecture and their eyes never moved from me. They just stared with cold, unblinking eyes. As my anxiety grew to a peak, I called class off early. I claimed that I was not feeling well, but no one seemed to care. They simply got up with robotic movements and left the classroom in silence.

As I traveled about the university that day, I recognized that I always had eyes on me. Whenever I looked over my shoulder or turned a new corner, I saw that there was always a student who stared at me with an unfeeling stare. I grew paranoid quickly.

This pattern repeated for days. I would be stared at constantly at the university. I refused to go back to my home, regardless of whether the police presumed that the area was safe. I knew they knew where I lived. I stopped staying at my sister's house, in fear that they would hurt her or my nieces, and moved to a rundown motel that allowed pets.

I knew who *they* were. *They* were my students. I had no way to prove it, but I knew. I told the Dean, but when he came to examine what I called "strange behavior" the students were miraculously back to normal. It was only after he left that they returned to their true and malicious selves. Colleagues started to look at me strangely and some students from my other courses would avoid me. I had gone from a relaxed man to one completely on edge. Gossip around campus was that I had "lost it." It was not *me* who had lost it. No! It was them! This torture went on for weeks. I started calling out of that deplorable class as much as possible, until the Dean forbade it. Nothing stopped my torment. Not missing class, not going home, not sleep. Nothing! They found me everywhere.

I lost my will to go to work when a severed arm appeared on my doorstep. I know not to whom it belonged. Instead, I sought out a man in Arkham who used to work for the university. He was a man of science until he found a love for the mystic. The university had deemed him unfit to teach due to his newfound preaching and forced him into early retirement.

I told him my whole story from the very beginning. This seemed to fill him with horror. He revealed to me the source of my plight: I had interrupted the ritual that the students were going to perform on poor Isis. This had angered the false god that they served, and he had taken away their souls rather than making them stronger. The only way for them to get their souls back was for them to sacrifice the one who had prevented their success. The old professor revealed to me that instead of physical torture, they had chosen torture that was psychological in nature. They would strike as I eventually broke down in screams of madness and anxiety.

There was also, unfortunately for me, no cure. They were possessed by their newly soulless bodies and would not relent until they retrieved what was taken from them. I was doomed.

I refused to believe this. I refused to believe that death was so near. In a desperate attempt for salvation, I returned to campus to seek the aid of the library. *The Necronomicon* had been returned. I flipped through the grimoire to find something, anything that could help.

The only spell I found was dastardly and I dared not consider it: how to destroy soulless beings.

I knew that I would never, could never do such a thing. Yet, I did not return *The Necronomicon*. Instead, I brought it with me to the class I had no intention of going to.

I saw the rest of this from an outsider perspective. I saw myself going through the motions, but I had no control of my own actions.

The students at their desks saw the book in my hands. That horrible, evil smirk came on Peter's face. Returning the book had been a test of my breaking will and anxiety. I had failed. They collectively moved slowly and threateningly forward towards me. I glared them down, my hand wavering as I opened the book and spoke those accursed, detestable words. All at once a green flame engulfed the room and the students started screaming, screaming unholy cries that I shall never forget. They ran about, frightened, but could not escape the flame. It was when the flame encumbered me that I fell unconscious.

When I awoke, I was in the hospital. The Dean as well as a doctor stood over me. I was lucky to be alive, they said. There had been a gas leak in the room, a fast-acting gas had inexplicably gotten into the lecture hall. It got in, killed all the students, and nearly killed me. They had no way of explaining how the gas got there, but the forensic squad had detected it.

Guilt sat in my throat as they spoke. I told them that I had done it. I had set the fire using *The Necronomicon* to kill them and I tried explaining my situation, but they stared at me blankly. They told me that I was delirious, that I needed to rest, that I had no idea what I was saying.

To this day no one believes me. No one. Not the police, not the university, no one. I could not bring myself to return. I quit my position not even two days before I was compelled to write this. I cannot live with this torment. I killed them all. They were in their prime, their golden years, and I snuffed them out. Why do I deserve life over them?

Susannah, my sweet sister, I leave Isis and Sammy to you. Take good care of them. Do not tell the girls their uncle went out this way.

Rainbow Connection

Have you ever thought about it? That thing, that force, that seems to tie humanity all together? Not just humanity—no. This is so much bigger than people. The stars, the very abyss of the ocean, even those caves you only see on the *Discovery Channel.*

All of it's connected.

You're lost—that's fine. But it all makes sense. You just have to look for it. No—not just that. You have to push your suspension of disbelief. Did you do it? Good.

Now, imagine the cosmos. You can't possibly see it all, not in that space you call your mind. It's unfathomable. An ant can't possibly begin to comprehend the backyard it lives in, only the tunnels it has created underground. What understanding do we have of something so infinite? None more than the ants—and we are even smaller in the grand scheme of things.

You might think you get it, but you don't.

You understand so far, right? Good.

Regardless, you can't help but look up at the stars in wonder as the autumn breeze brushes against your cheeks. You smile as you imagine you see pictures in the lights spilled across the black void.

"There's the Big Dipper," you say, squinting as you try to make certain. You're never certain.

Why are you so drawn to this smattering of stars across the sky? You're never certain about that either. Just as you're not sure why the deep ocean or those recesses beneath the earth are appealing. You see them in those documentaries: the Vampire Squid from Hell, the stalactites with drops of water falling into underground lakes. You see a blind white lizard climb up from the lake's ooze, and you squirm. You sit transfixed as the vampire squid's bioluminescent display precedes its disappearance into the Twilight Zone. Do your research, the dark depths of the ocean are *really* called that.

Why do you need to know about these things? Things that have absolutely no bearing on your day-to-day life, things that you're never likely to encounter within your lifetime? These things are so different, but they evoke the same feelings in you: They're provocative, alluring. Tempting.

Make sure you write this down.

You want to see the squid, the lizard, the Big Dipper.

Why?

Because they are out of your reach. Because they are not meant for you, and yet, they call you. They demand to be discovered, explored, named. It's in your nature to want to conquer them, devour what you can learn.

Confused?

Take the child's explanation. Do you know "Rainbow Connection?" Kermit the Frog sings it, and so does Willie Nelson, as a matter of fact.

What's so amazing that keeps us stargazing, and what do we think we might see?

You know the rest. But what *is* so amazing that you are called to the heavens, the sea, the pits of the Earth? Is *amazing* even the right word?

No.

Did you write that down?

You're confused again, this is becoming too abstract.

What else do all of these places, these wonders (fools will mistakenly call them this) have in common?

Danger.

This force, this natural curiosity instilled inside you is your very own siren. She means to bring you crashing into the rocks one way or another.

Is this the sweet sound that calls the young sailors? The voice might be one and the same.

The deep sea — you can't reach it, the pressure is too great. Besides, you wouldn't be able to hold your breath long enough to get there.

The stars — your bones will be scraping against the ceiling of your own anti-gravitational coffin by the time you reach them.

Caves — so easy to get lost. Most have noxious fumes. It's no place for you to sip your coffee as you ogle up at the bats. Besides, you don't want to get guano in your shoes.

Don't you see? Some force of nature, maybe inside of you, maybe around you, is pulling you towards your doom. As you chase after what you don't know, what you were never meant to know, what you yearn to discover, you are brought that much closer to your death.

Every day, people come up with new innovations to try and reach the unreachable — submarines, rockets, the list goes on.

Every day, people romanticize this siren. It's a call to adventure, the rainbow connection.

You can see it, can't you?

Allow one last argument. You've read *The Bible*, yes?

Of course you have.

Then you know that the rainbow is a sign from God, a promise that He will never try to flood the earth again. He will never try to drown out mankind again. That's the Rainbow Covenant. But what if He could urge you to drown yourself by attempting to explore the depths? What if He could eradicate mankind through their own nature? Their own siren's song? This truth — this Faustian urge we have for knowledge, the folly that comes from it, is recognized, even if unconsciously. Why else call it the rainbow connection?

What's that?

Time's up? So it is!

Thank you for listening, Doc. Same time next week?

Perfect.

Bye.

Boogeyman

I sit on my couch and my skin freezes. Those eyes. I know those eyes. Where have I seen them? Not here. I haven't seen this show before, but something about those eyes, that face, those vacant pockets force me to look.

Serial killer. I would know it if they didn't tell me what he was, what he had done, because it was all in the eyes. It's a cliché that all serial killers have dead eyes, no emotion behind them, just coal wedged between bones. I would know this face in a lineup of thousands. The evil radiating from him awakens some dormant, automatic fear within me, something innate. I don't believe in such things, but it happened.

Logical explanation? I've seen him in a dream. Dreams are generally carefully preserved in my memory, reflected upon in the morning, shared, then forgotten. My mom once told me, after a nightmare where my father was hacked into pieces by a mummy, that the only way to destroy a bad dream is to tell it to someone. This takes away its power.

I can't find satisfaction in this explanation, as my dreams won't let me remember this man, in spite of my dreams molding around his presence. *It*—not his or him. How can *It* be a *he* when only presented in a void of remembrance, an amorphous blob of violence and death? I don't like to think about *It*. In fact, I can remember dreams in which I completely denied *Its* existence. I'm safe in Dreamworld, where I have subconscious control.

Not in reality. There *It* shows up as the police sketch of Richard Ramirez. I'd like to think the picture was foreign to me, but dream logic dictates that I can't make *It* up. Dreams pull from reality.

The sketch artist portrays Ramirez as vague as my dreams. The Night Stalker is drawn with a gaunt, triangular face. The hair on his head is brown, but I can't figure out the hair-type from the sketch. It looks as though the artist dipped a sponge in brown paint, pressing it to his sketch like a kindergarten art project. It's not any of this that startles me. Not even the stabbing eyes provoke fear, though I have never been a fan of the uncanny. It's the story I know that comes with them, the story I hide from, even in my dreams. I'm haunted in reality by the boogeyman.

The dream is clear. I hate repeating myself, but this is important. It plays out like a movie, just for me, a movie that I have the feeling is based on a fictional dream book I've never read. I can see the girl with obsidian curls flowing over her shoulders, her hips swaying in step as she walks home. This woman is a reporter, looking for the same man — no, same *thing* — who stalks her. She finds *It*. Police kick down the front door. *Its* house is one I know from childhood, belonging to my mom's friend, Mark, who had many trinkets inherited from his father I enjoyed looking at. This sweet memory is now tainted. Rather than spectacles and inherited books from Mark's father, I see *It* holding a knife to Reporter-Woman. *It* lets her go to show the police something. In a cubby under the staircase is a corpse wrapped in once white linen. It is now stained with crusty brown and light green slime. It makes a sound like a wet sponge as he jostles his neatly wrapped package. This is *Its* mother, and *It* can't bear the secret being out. The knife turns on its owner, the tip jamming just under the eyelid. Blood streams down *Its* cheeks in mockery of tears. *It* cuts upward, through the eye, then around, carving a jack-o-lantern in Its own face, before pulling it out and starting on the next eye. *It* never stopped laughing, even though the screams.

Now *It* found me in reality.

I tremble as I'm told Ramirez gouged the eyes from one of his victims. I pause the show. My stomach churns. What do I do? How do I make *It* go away?

Mom once told me that you can take the power away from a nightmare by telling someone about it. Repetition is bad writing, but this is important.

I sit.

I take the power away from the *Thing* that pervades day and night in the only form that encompasses thought and subconscious.

I write.

You have no more power.

Go away.

Cold Calling

The newfound prominence of streaming services made Verizon's employees flinch at the upraised fist of layoffs. A decrease in subscriptions meant a decrease in available positions. Luke Martin Daniels' seniority gave him the opportunity to cry tears not dissimilar to that of a black widow at the funeral of her late husband. Both his job and his new hobby remained secure.

The Verizon van stalked the McClellan household from the Gorbinski's front yard. This neighborhood was borderless. Manicured lawn seeped into manicured lawn. Hedges stood guard before suburbia's trademark white picket fences in trimmed conformity. A Verizon disk played peek-a-boo from behind the McClellan chimney. The adjacent driveway was empty.

It was five p.m. and still no sign of Jody McClellan. Daniels reached into the pocket of his black polo shirt and pulled out a *Five Star* memo pad. He flipped through the pages until he found McClellan written atop the page's first blue line in blocky lettering. The notes written below had the resemblance of doctor's scrawl; hurriedly written in nonsensical squiggles. Daniels squinted.

> *McClellan*
> *Boys and husband gone since Monday.*
> *No dog.*
> *Leave home ~ 6am*
> *Return ~ 4:30pm*
> *Remain awake till 10pm*
> *Silver Toyota [find make]*

What's taking her so long?

Daniels replaced the memo pad and stared at his dashboard. 5:15 blinked back at him in white blocks. WKPX's throwback channel crooned Blue Öyster Cult's "(Don't Fear) The Reaper." His fingers fell against the center console's torn felt cover in the style of a wave, one touching the surface after the next. His index finger probed a tear in the fabric, tracing circles on the plastic interior. Motion in the McClellan window caught his eye. A curtain brushed the window screen's wire mesh before falling motionless.

So she is home.

Daniels reached into the back seat. His son's duffle bag was on the floor, covering his tool kit. He hoisted the bag onto the passenger seat. The baseball bat and water bottle made a discordant C sharp as they clanged together. The smell of mud and Axe wafted upwards. The toolbox was on its side, wedged between the seat and the floor. As Daniels moved it, its contents shifted, tilting the box towards him. There was no clang, only a soft thump.

The door slammed. The resounding *thump* bounded through the neighborhood, but remained unacknowledged. As he stalked toward the house, he felt his phone vibrate in his jeans pocket. He switched the toolbox to his left hand.

5:05 *Lilly*
Don't forget to drive Brayden to baseball practice after work.

Damn bitch. Now I have to rush.

5:16 *Me*
ok babe love u

Work boots padded against the sidewalk as he made his approach. Just before the walkway, which was lined with mums, Daniels looked left and right. About five houses down, a young boy rode a battery-powered Lightning McQueen up and down the driveway. His father watched the bottom of his *Heineken* bottle, oblivious to the cable man. In the corner of his vision, he noticed the curtains tango with the window sill once more.
Why not just open up the door?
He moved up the walkway. As soon as his boot hit the first step, the front door opened.
"What took ya so long?"
Daniels looked up into the gray eyes of Jody McClellan. Her dahlia lips curled upwards into a china-doll smile. Her shoulder rested on the doorframe, her left hand in the outermost jeans pocket.
"There's no car in the driveway."
Jody brushed a brown sugar strand away from her cheek. "I parked in the garage." She shifted her weight onto her back leg and motioned with her thumb into the house. "D'ya still have time?"
"Time for what?"
Jody tilted her head down and to the side as if posing for an

unseen *JCPenney* photographer. "You aren't here to check my boxes?"

"Well, no." Daniels squeezed the handle of his toolbox tighter. "This is just a courtesy call. To see if you're happy with your service, what we can do to keep you on board, all that stuff."

Jody hummed. "I coulda swore we made some kinda appointment."

Daniels shrugged.

"Well, c'mon in."

Jody retreated inside the house, but Daniels found himself hesitating. He pulled out his phone. The time, 5:20, was framed just above the heads of his wife and son. She stood behind him, arms around his neck, chin rested atop his head. She dyed her hair often, but little gray hairs protruded from her scalp. Brayden looked coolly unamused, but a smile betrayed him. He looked much like a younger version of his father, back when he still had the ladies lined up and a full head of hair. His hairline retreated halfway across his skull in his 30s. He was lucky to have black strands covering the back of his head, but he often wondered if it would be better to shave it off.

"Are ya coming?" Jody called. "I can grab ya some ice-tea, if ya want?"

"That'd be nice." Daniels entered the house. The doorway opened into a living room, a staircase to his immediate left. A black leather couch and matching loveseat faced one another in the room's center. In the middle was a glass coffee table, a laptop square in the center, and some *Magic Treehouse* books spread around it. One had a bookmark made of loose-leaf paper. Toys were scattered about, a truck here, a *Nerf* gun there. The room did not have a TV. Candles were everywhere with scents ranging from "Spring Beach" to "Christmas Cookie." There was a strange odor underneath he couldn't identify, but with all of these scents mixing, he was experiencing sensory overload.

The far wall was decorated with a big wooden sign saying, "Home is where the rugrats are," with pictures of the family surrounding it. Jody and her husband stood proudly before the altar on their wedding day in one photo. Her hand rested against his chest. Next to this was a picture of the two boys. One held a Mickey Mouse fishing pole with a two-inch bait fish dangling from the hook. His eyes were squeezed shut and his smile took up much of his face. The younger boy looked at the ground, arms crossed, and without a fishing pole. "These your boys?"

"Mhm. Aren't they cyooot?" Ice cubes clanged against the class. "D'ya want sugar in it?"

"Unsweetned's okay, thanks."

Daniels cast a glance at the kitchen. The house was an open plan concept, so one room flowed into the next with little interruption. A mahogany dinner table stood in the center of the next room; four chairs placed in the center of each side. They all had red cushions, but only one had a blue booster seat strapped onto it. The dining room was separated from the kitchen by an island. Jody stood with her back to the living room. He could hear the ice-tea waterfall into the glasses. He set his toolbox down on the coffee table and flicked open the two front facing clasps. Inside, rather than wires and screwdrivers were zip ties, handcuffs, silver duct tape, rope, and a gun. He took out his handcuffs and ran his thumb along the ridged edge.

"You have any kids?" Jody's footsteps were getting louder.

He closed his toolbox and shoved the cuffs into his pocket. "Just the one. His name's Brayden."

"Here ya go," Jody extended a glass with Sonic's face etched in the side. "Sorry, all of my big boy cups are in the dishwasher."

"I get it. Thank you." Daniels smiled. He took a sip of his drink. The ice sloshed upwards and brushed against his upper lip. His wispy mustache was drenched, so he used the back of his hand to clean it off.

"You have a picture of your son?" Jody tilted her head like she had outside.

It's performative, that's what it is. She's playing sweet for the cable guy. "Yeah." He pulled his phone from his pocket, clicked the center button, and turned to show her the home screen.

5:25. I have to move soon.

"Awwwwwww. He looks just like you."

"Yeah, me in the 90's maybe."

A polite smile graced Jody's lips before she brought her ice-tea to her mouth.

"Listen, I'd love to chat all day, but I want to take a look at your TV set up. Make sure all's running well before we talk logistics."

"Just wanna jump right in, huh?" Jody chuckled. "Tell ya what.

Finish your ice-tea while I switch my laundry loads, then I'll show ya the TV. There's one in my room, and one in the boy's room."

Daniels smiled. He watched Jody head back to the kitchen as he brought the glass back to his lips. He channeled mankind's distant kinship with the whale to swallow the iced tea in one gulp. He looked around for a coaster, but eventually settled on placing the glass on the coffee table directly. Then he waited. And waited. And waited. The clock read 5:35.

How long does it take to put in a fucking load of laundry?

The sides of Daniels' head began to pound. He pushed his hand down into his left pocket and ran his thumb over the serrated edge of the cuffs. Over and over and over.

After I drop Brayden off, I'm taking a nap. I deserve it after this shit.

The headache started to seem like a migraine. The lights were too bright. If he moved the wrong way, he swore the walls would imitate a Lazy Susan. It was then that Jody reemerged.

"Sorry, I ran to the bathroom real fast too." Jody walked past him to the staircase without stopping. "C'mon, I'll take ya to the one in my room first."

Fina-fucking-ly.

Daniels refused to lift his feet, opting to shuffle them along the carpet. The floor threatened to drop from around him, just like that carnival ride where people get stuck to the walls. Brayden loved that one. It was called *The Cyclone* at the Summer Fun-Fair.

The adrenaline will kick in. That's what happens.

The upstairs was dark. Jody made no attempt to turn on the lights and Daniels was thankful. A room at the end of the hallway had the lights on. It cast golden spaghetti strands across the rug. The sudden promise of bright light blackmailed him with a migraine. The smell of old socks and wet clothes grew as he followed Jody. When they got there, Jody twisted the knob, but the door didn't budge. She tried again, this time placing her shoulder against it.

"Oh, shit, I must've locked it. Will ya give it a shot?"

Daniels frowned. "Sure." He tried the knob and pushed inwards, but something was blocking the way.

Is it clothes? Downstairs was clean enough. Doesn't seem like she'd be a slob.

He put his shoulder into it and the door gave out automatically. Something thumped against the carpet, but he had no time to process that, as the bed trapped his attention. A woman's wrist was handcuffed to the left side of the bed with one pink fuzzy handcuff. Her head sat on the night table next to her, a scream molded onto it, brown sugar hair mussed with blood. On the right side of the bed was a man, presumably the husband, his right wrist cuffed in matching pink. It almost seemed as though he was looking upwards, but Daniels soon noticed the only thing holding the head on was its position and chunks of ragged flesh. He had to swim through the air in order to take a step into the room. The walls encircled him. Something came down on the back of his head, and he greeted the ground with limp arms.

***

Daniels woke up to someone patting his cheek gently. The first thing he saw were the boys. The elder slumped in front of the door, one hand stretched out before him. His *Batman* pajamas were covered in a flaky dark brown, much like the carpet beneath him. The younger boy was curled against the wall in a fetal position. His *Paw Patrol* pants were wet with urine and blood. The whole room smelled of sour eggs. No candles in here. He wanted to gag, but he found that he couldn't, as duct tape pressed against his lips. His hands were cuffed in metal and brushed against those of the corpses. His back was wet with sweat and blood. He could feel some dripping down his neck, but he knew most of it would be from the corpses beside him.

"It was nice of ya to share your toys."

Daniels lulled his head to the side. Jody — *not Jody, who the fuck is she?* — held his toolbox next to her head and rattled it. Her china doll smile burned into him. It was so impassive, so cold.

"Mmpfh. Mmmhrm."

"Can't understand ya." The woman let the toolbox fall to the ground as she approached the bedside. "This'll help."

Half the hairs from his mustache were pulled off as the tape was removed. It was promptly replaced with her hand. He bit down. Her head cocked to the side; the hand remained unmoving. She eventually pulled it away to examine and tilted it downward to watch the blood trickle. She licked it.

"Who... Who the fuck are you?"

She bared her pristine pearl teeth. "Wouldn't *you* like to know?"

"I... I saw Jody. I saw her walk in and out—"

"You're quite the busy bee." She reached into Daniel's chest pocket and pulled out his memo pad. "Let's see who's in your appointment book, hm? You've got Smith, Rutherford, Ramierez, Oakenbaum, and then the McClellans. But none of those other folks are dead, are they?"

Daniels shook his head. As his head moved to the right, he saw a maggot crawl from Mr. McClellan's neck.

"You watch all these gals at once?"

"Yes."

She put the memo pad into her pocket. "So, there were times you *weren't* watching Jody, right? When you were just lookin' at the others?"

"I'd guess so."

"Well, isn't it possible that during one of those times, Mr. McClellan came home with the boys while you weren't looking? That I nabbed your prey right out from under your nose?"

"I've seen her leave for work every day—"

"EHHH," she mimicked the sound of a buzzer. "You've seen *me* leave every day."

"What'd you do at her job for all that time?"

"I work—sorry—*worked* with her. I noticed ya tailing her a month ago. Man, it was interesting watching ya do your thing. A little killer in the making." The woman sunk to her knees, humming a tune he couldn't recognize as she flipped open the toolbox's locks. *Snap, snap.* "You have some nice toys here. How many did ya think you'd need, hm?"

"I wanted to be sure I had—"

"Had what? A back-up plan?" When she stood back up, she held his gun in her hand. Daniels noticed for the first time that she now wore gloves. "Or options?"

"I dunno. Both." Daniels bit his inner lip.

"Both? Hmm... First time?" She smiled and poked his nose with the barrel. "How cute. Lemme guess, you're still figuring out what you like? How ya'd like to kill me?"

"Listen, I—I didn't even know it was you." She cocked the gun. The sting of sweat made it hard to keep his eyes open. "Let's just forget it. I'll go home, and... we can forget all of this."

"Bang." She moved the gun upwards as she mimicked a shot, before bringing down the barrel on his head. Sweat mixed with blood, tinging his lips with the taste of salty pennies.

He screamed, but his attacker didn't seem to notice. She instead slipped back down to the ground. *Snap, snap, clang.* The gun was back in the toolbox. "It can be hard, y'know? Finding what excites ya. That's why I never thought about it, like you did. I've got my own methods."

Daniels cast a gaze to the window. It was night. Brayden wouldn't get to baseball practice. The van wouldn't be returned. *Someone will notice I'm gone. Someone will come looking for me. It's only a matter of time.* "Why would you kill someone so close?"

She popped up with rope in her hands.

"You don't think they'll piece it together? You didn't think *that* through, did you?"

The woman crawled onto the bed, over the body of Jody McClellan.

"The smell. How has no one smelled it yet? Someone will catch you on smell alone."

Daniels writhed beneath her as she climbed atop him, straddling his hips with her thighs.

"You're going to get blood on you. How are you going to explain that?" His hands jiggled their chains, brushing his skin against that of his intended victims. A tear rolled down his cheek.

"They'll come looking for me. They're probably already looking for me right now. You hear that. They-" A leather coated finger pressed against his lips.

"I know this was gonna be your first murder, so I'll let ya in on a little secret." She leaned down, soft locks tickling against his upper lip, now coated in sweat and mucus. She breathed in his ear. "Sometimes, ya just can't help yourself, and ya gotta go with the flow."

Her hands flew to his neck, thumb pressing into his Adam's apple. She squeezed. Daniels kicked, twisted, and turned. Nothing. His eyes bulged from his skull as he stared up at her. Her flower petal lips never moved. Just as the edges of his vision went black, she let go. Daniels gasped for air. The woman pushed her hands down on his chest. "That would've been too easy, hon. Ya know the drill, I want *my* fun, too."

Daniels felt a buzz against his thigh. She seemed to notice too, as she promptly reached down for his phone.

6:20 Lilly
Were r u
6:30 Lilly
U better have a good reason for this
6:31 Lilly
Were tf are u Luke
15 missed messages
10 missed calls
7:49 Lilly
Luke r u okay
7:50 Lilly
i luv u

Her smile fell. "I don't think we have time to play anymore." She took the rope from the space between her thigh and Jody McClellan and tied it around his neck. And she pulled. And pulled. Daniels flailed helplessly.

My God, not like this.

Crack.

The woman dropped the rope on Daniel's chest and returned her attention to his phone. She used his emergency dial function to call 911 and left the operator to speak with death laden air. Jody pulled the memo pad from her pocket. She flipped through the pages as she walked down the stairs, humming.

Till Death Do Us Part

"You want me to put a walking *corpse* on stand?"

"I really wish you'd stop calling him that." Vince twirled a pen in his hand. His fingers worked effortlessly, never missing a beat, like they were at the loom. No thought was required, it was as natural as brushing his teeth or stomping on a spider in the kitchen. He leaned back in his steel chair. His unbranded sneakers hooked around the bolted legs. He tugged at the collar of his orange jumpsuit, which was buttoned up to the collar, every minute or so. Although his collar was tight, the jumpsuit draped over him like an ocean wave. "His name's Adam."

Frank Fitz gripped the bridge of his nose. "Fine, Adam. Look, bringing him to the stand is what we are fighting *against*."

"I don't get it. He'd be testifying *for us*." The pen ducked behind his middle finger before being caught by his ring finger. "Don't you think it'd be helpful to show the audience he's not pulled straight off *The Walking Dead*?"

"Doesn't matter. The second—" Fitz groaned. "Will you stop doing that and pay attention?"

"Doing what?"

"The *pen*. It's distracting me."

"Sorry." He caught the pen with his pinky as it came behind the former two fingers. He then pushed it into his palm with his thumb. The pen clicked once, twice, before it rested on the stainless-steel tabletop.

"The second he, or you, acknowledges that you knew he was dead, they're gonna slam you with that verdict."

"He was never even a *corpse*, Frank. How are they gonna get me on desecration? His dad pulled him together from a bunch of different people—corpses—whatever the fuck we're calling them."

"You don't know that. You *can't* know that if we're going to win this thing." Fitz sighed. "Mr. Halloway, we should really be working on your testimony."

Vince shrugged. "You're the boss."

Frank stood, pulling down his grey blazer. He adjusted the cuffs on his wrists before looking up to his client. "Mr. Halloway, when did you meet the victim?"

Vince crossed his arms over his chest. The oversized sleeves of his jumpsuit hung down like an old woman's arms. "He's not a victim."

"Please play along, Mr. Halloway."

"Fine, fine. A year and a half ago, I think."

Fitz walked toward the two-way glass before walking back to the table. "Where did you meet him?"

"Tinder."

Fitz continued his walk. Back and forth. "How long did you talk with the victim before meeting him face to face?"

"A few days, maybe a week." Vince's green eyes followed Fitz, his thumb rubbed gently up and down his bicep, sinking through the fabric to find his arm.

"How long until your relationship became intimate?"

"We met on Tinder, Frank." Vince raised his brows. "Pretty much as soon as we met in person."

"When you met him in person, did you notice anything… off about him?"

"No."

"The scars weren't off-putting?" Fitz raised his brows, which invaded his would-be hairline.

Vince shrugged. "They weren't my business."

"But you did see them?"

"Sure."

"All of them?" His brows rose even higher.

"What part of *we met on Tinder* don't you get?"

"Mr. Halloway, please." His eyebrows fell, crocheting together. "Try to be professional."

"Sorry, yes, I saw all of them."

"And they weren't suspicious to you?"

"Like I said, they weren't my business."

"Did the victim eventually tell you where he got the scars from?"

"Yes."

"And what did he say?"

"They're from when his dad put him together."

Frank slid his hand down his face, starting where his eyebrows rested to his chin. His hand lingered by his mouth for a moment, covering his thin, boardwalk plank lips, before dropping it to his side. "I told you; you *can't* know this."

"I'm not adding perjury to this bullshit."

"Just tell a half-truth. Say..." Fitz's lips disappeared into his mouth once more. "Say that they're from birth."

"And when they ask for specifics?" The bottom right of Vince's lip indented as he bit down. "How do I get around that?"

"Birth defects."

"He doesn't have any of those. He's *perfect* just the way he is." Vince sat up in his chair, pressing his palms against the cool, metal seat. "Isn't it just easier to tell the truth? I didn't do anything wrong!"

Fitz raked his bottom lip with his teeth, momentarily revealing *Claire*'s bubblegum nail polish color inside, before it disappeared with a *pop*. "That might work. We could plead insanity and—"

Vince slammed his hands against the table. "I'm *not* crazy! Nothing about Adam's illegal, at least on my part. He's of age, he's alive, he's consenting."

"Is he of age? I mean, he must have been made only—"

"Get out!" Vince stood, stumbling before catching his balance with the table. "I've had enough of this shit for one day."

Frank's hands slipped into his pockets. "We'll figure out how to talk around that next time, okay? I didn't mean to get you fired up."

"I wouldn't be *fired up* if you did what I'm paying you for."

"You don't pay me, the state does." Fitz put a hand on his client's shoulder. He made an indent in the fabric, the orange cloth billowing up like a feather pillow around him. His eyebrows raised again. "I'm trying to give you the best help I can, but I can't do that if you won't let me. Let's just pick this up tomorrow, huh?"

Vince remained silent.

Fitz moved his hand to clap his client on the back, before moving out the door.

"He's all yours, boys." The prison guards stood up straighter as they heard the lawyer's voice, though the performance was unnecessary. He hardly looked their way.

***

"You get one phone call."

"Y'know, I always thought that was a myth."

Kathy snorted air from her nose. "They always do."

The divot in Vince's lip reappeared. His eyes scanned over the buttons, which jutted up from the silver box like teeth. The black, plastic phone lay in the receiver. "I haven't memorized a number since the 2000s."

"I have a list of approved numbers for you in the office."

"That'd be great." Vince's smile matched the shackles around his ankles. "Thanks."

Kathy shook her head. "Yeah." As she moved away from him, her shoes click-clacked against the linoleum. "Stay put or the boys outside will taze you."

Vince nodded. Kathy's blonde ponytail swayed side to side with each step. *Click.* The door closed behind her. Vince listened to the clacks of her footsteps become muted by the phone's hum. He didn't know which room she had to go to, or how long she'd be. This put urgency behind his fingers as he dialed. The four was stuck and required extra force. Then he waited. And waited.

"Hello?"

"Adam," Vince wheezed. "It's me."

It took Adam a while to respond, not because the words wouldn't come to him, but because each was wrapped in decision. "I didn't think they'd let you call."

"They didn't, they don't." Vince swallowed. "Kathy left me alone for a minute, I don't have a lot of time."

Adam's brows knit together, the *clack-clack* of the needles audible over the phone. "You're aware these calls are recorded, right?"

"I don't care. I mean, they can't go through *all* of them, right?"

"*All* of the prisoners don't call simultaneously. This is a bad idea, Vince, you could—"

"Shut up." His voice clipped like a toenail, with jagged edges. "I mean, don't shut up. I just… I needed to talk to you, even if it's only for a minute."

"Parting is such sweet sorrow." Adam learned to speak through books, so quotes came the fastest to Adam, his own twirling pen.

"Stop being so corny. It's a waste of time." Vince listened as his lover's breathy laugh filled the receiver. "You're probably the only person who read *Romeo and Juliet* outside high school. Hell, most just *pretend* to read it in high school."

Silence reigned. It was difficult to differentiate the continuous hum of Adam's breathing from that of the line.

"They subpoenaed me," Adam hummed.

"Who? Frank?"

Click-clack go the needles. "Who's Frank?"

"My lawyer."

"No, no… It was Ms. Costella. She's the prosecutor."

"Figures. Y'know, I tried to get Frank to subpoena you, but he said it was a bad idea."

"He's correct, I think. The jury will take one look and me and they'll–"

"And then they'll hear you talk and how eloquent you are. Or they'll see your eyes and all the thoughts behind them. Or… or hear your sighs and… God, I miss you."

"You *just* chided me for being sappy, Vin."

"Don't make me regret it."

Clump, clump. Boots marched against linoleum like a tinker toys robotic eternal gate. "I have to go, Adam. I… Parting is such sweet sorrow."

"Love you too."

Vince put down the receiver. A butterfly flew from his stomach in a sigh and his organs tried for their Knot-Tying Badge.

Click. "Got that list." Kathy waved the ripped notebook paper in a parody of a flag ending a race. "Who do you want to call?"

***

"The prosecution would like to call Mr. Adam to the stand."

Adam rose. He had been seated behind the prosecution, but now he stood like a cable-tower. He wore a Yankees baseball cap on his head, permitted by the judge, to hide his scars. This did nothing, however, to hide his green eyes. One was slightly more pronounced, like that of a goldfish, ready to pop from his skull. His face had the least amount of visible stitching. He was a collage; pale skin here, dark skin there. Vince loved to trace the borders. Black hair dripped from his hat like rain. Most of it was pulled back into a bun, but the rest sat on his head, a perilous yarn hank. His left arm was shorter than his right, which he hid by walking sideways, edging past an invisible crowd. The sleeves of his blazer rested by his elbows, while the sleeves of his collared shirt fell just above his wrists. As he raised his right hand, the sleeves moved down further.

"Do you swear to tell the truth, the whole truth, and nothing but the truth, so help you God?" The man who asked this came only to Adam's breast. He held the book far away from him with *La-Z-Boy* arms.

"I do." When Adam sat, the courtroom let out a collective sigh. Adam adjusted his sleeves.

The prosecutor rose. She wore a pin-striped blazer and skirt combo with a *Land-o-Lakes* half-and-half blouse underneath. Her heels stabbed the wooden floors as she moved forward. The jury watched her, some looking for marks on the floor. "Mr. Adam... Do you have a last name?"

Adam shrugged. "Not legally, no."

"You don't keep your father's last name?"

"I have many fathers." Adam lifted a hand and gestured to his face. "I've never made a point to track down the parentage of my donors."

"I should be clearer. Your... creator. You didn't take his last name?"

"No."

"Why not?"

"He committed suicide as soon as he saw me move."

Someone in the jury box whispered to their neighbor. Vince slumped in his seat.

Ms. Costella moved to stand in front of her desk and leaned back on it. "How old are you, Adam?"

"It's hard to say. Father used various parts, but I believe my brain is from a thirty-year-old."

"That's not what I mean." A heel brushed against the floor as the prosecutor crossed her legs. "How long have you, *Adam*, been alive?"

"Eight years."

"So, legally speaking, you're a child?"

Adam squinted his good eye. The other remained open. "Do I look eight years old? Sound it?"

"Objection," Fitz called. He half stood, not pushing the chair far enough away to demand his full height. The lawyer posed to dive into his files. Vince tilted his head to inspect his lawyer. "Argumentative."

"Sustained." The judge, who sat directly beside Adam, kept his sandbag laden eyes locked on Costella. His voice dripped with command and liquid sugar. "Try to remember who's on trial here, Ms. Costella."

She nodded automatically. "When did you meet Mr. Halloway?"

"A year and a half ago."

"So, you were alone for six and a half years?"

"That sounds right."

"And who took care of you in those six years?"

"Well…" Adam looked up to the ceiling. "I did."

"How admirable." Costella crossed her arms over her chest. "How did you do that? Teach yourself, I mean?"

"It's complicated. In the way anybody learns."

"I see." As Costella nodded her head, a strand of brown hair fell in her face. She made no effort to move it. "And you were with the corpse of your father the whole time?"

"No. It was removed."

"How did you know to call the police? If you were just born, that is?"

Vince nudged Fitz. His lawyer shrugged.

"I didn't. Someone found him."

"Who was that?"

Adam slumped in his chair. "I don't remember."

Costella pushed herself off of the desk and looped around it. "I would like to present both yourself, and the jury, with Exhibit A." She pulled a sandwich bag from her briefcase, which was on top of her chair. In lieu of the prosecutor's lunch was a photograph and *Exhibit A* written in black sharpie across the top. The dots of the 'i's were smudged. One of the figures in the picture was Vince. His dark, brown curls nestled the neck of someone taller. He was still wiry, but the other person looked a wisp in comparison. His dark hair was somehow wilder although it was straight. The first two buttons of his collared shirt were undone. Stubble polluted his face in clusters, refusing to grow uniformly. He looked like he was pulled from a black-and-white flick in comparison to Vince's vibrance. His tanned, olive complexion made the man beside him look like a specter. His shirt was cerulean with multicolored dinosaurs. The photo was then presented to Adam. "Recognize these two?"

Adam took the photo in his hand. "This is a photo of Vince and my father."

"Did you know the two knew one another?"

"Yes. Vince was a student of his, I believe."

"Would it surprise you to know they were dating?" Costella moved behind her desk again.

"Objection!" Fitz prepared his dive. "Relevance?"

"I'll allow it." The liquid sugar dripped. "Go ahead, Ms. Costella."

Adam's lips pursed, causing the sliver of pale rosé skin to disappear. "They weren't dating."

"Would you like to read Exhibit B aloud then?" She pulled a piece of paper from her briefcase. "I think it's only fair that you learn the truth."

Vince sunk downward, stopped only by a nudge from Fitz.

Adam took the paper from Costella as soon as she presented it. "Where am I reading?"

"The highlighted portion."

He cleared his throat. "June 8th, 2013." Adam looked to Vince. Tears pounded against the latter's eyes, demanding freedom. "Vince; hey. Are you busy? Stern; Working on a project. Stern; Can you wait? Vince; waited forever already. Meet me at our bar. Stern; We've been to lots. Which one? Vince; Really? Vince..." Adam paused, closing his eyes. The lids only came down halfway on the goldfish eye. "Do I have to read this?"

"Please." Costella crossed her arms.

"Vince; the one where we–" The paper cracked beneath his fingers. "You were sleeping with my *father*?"

The judge cut in. "Mr. Adam, you must–"

"It was *nine years ago*! Adam, it was before I met you, before you were even *around*. You've gotta understand–"

Fitz nudged his client to silence.

Costella clicked her tongue against the roof of her mouth. "I understand, Adam, why you feel the need to defend him. Mr. Halloway must have done a lot for you, am I right?"

"I love him. That's more than enough for me to speak on his behalf."

A tear fell down Vince's cheek. He mouthed *"I love you, too."* Adam's gaze remained on the attorney.

"That's sweet." Costella smiled with vinegar. "How long have you been together?"

"A year and a half."

"And where did you meet?"

"Tinder."

"Where did you get the phone?"

"Objection." The papers rustled in preparation for Fitz's splash.

"Relevance?"

"Sustained. Go on, Ms. Costella." *Drip, drip.*

"Well… It was my father's. He couldn't use it anymore, obviously, so I took it."

"And who taught you how to use it?"

"I taught myself."

Costella hummed. She strolled over to a computer on the side of the courtroom and wiggled the mouse. "I'd like to present the jury with Exhibit C. This was taken from Mr. Stern's phone."

A text conversation appeared on a projector screen, reading:

Dec. 4th 2014
Me: fud
Vince: fud? Food?
Me: food
Vince: Hungry?
Me: yEs s
Vince: OK, I'll get some. Stay.
Me: y Es

"Does this look like one and a half years ago, Adam?"

"Objection!" Fitz stands fully this time. "Argumentative."

"Sustained. Watch it, Ms. Costella."

"Unless I'm mistaken, Adam, you two *have* met earlier, unless, of course, your father forgot how to type?"

Adam looked at Vince. His orange jumpsuit had fresh, pea-sized blotches. "He found me there when Father committed suicide. He told me later, when I was more… cognizant… that he was a student of my father's."

Costella nodded. "He's done a lot for you then."

"He did."

"Is that why you started dating?"

"No."

"Why then?"

"Why does anyone get together?"

"I misspoke. Tell us *how* you got together then."

The rosé skin disappeared once more. "We were speaking one day and… One thing led to another."

"What did you talk about?"

"The world, what they must think of me. I told him what I thought and then…" A smile cut through his cheeks. "He told me what he thought of me."

"And then you got together?"

"Yes."

"Did you know anything about relationships? Sex?"

"Not through experience, but-"

"Would you agree that there was an imbalance of power?"

"No."

"You don't think so?" Costella moved from the projector to the witness stand. The floor cried out in clicks with each stab of her heel. "He raised you, taught you, and fed you. That's not an imbalance of power? Not even when he was your only human contact? Don't you think he was using his power over you to get what he wanted?"

Fitz made an effort to stand, but Adam was quick to answer. "I wanted it too."

"Did you? Or did he make you think that?"

"No, I wanted it, too. He made me *feel* alive, feel *human*, feel *wanted*. Is that a crime?"

"When you're not human? Yes."

A tear rolled down Adam's cheek as a boom came from the defense table. Vince was now standing, hands pressed against the table. Emotion overtook his speech like a getaway car. His chair flew away from behind him and into the audience barrier with a *thunk*. "That's enough! He's more human than any of you. I'll bet he's wiser, smarter, more caring-"

The gavel roared. "Mr. Halloway, you need to be seated *now*." The sugar disappeared from his voice.

"I've sat here and listened to her grill him long enough. Yes, I lied, and I'm sorry, Adam, but I thought… I love you. I was being selfish, but I…"

Adam stood. "Vince, I—I'm not mad, I promise, I—"

The gavel screamed. "Both of you sit before I hold you in contempt of court."

"Do it! I can't watch you do this to him—to us—anymore. We haven't—" Vince was quieted by the bailiff pulling his hands behind his back.

Adam, now seated, watched as they pulled his boyfriend away. The door echoed behind the pair as they left.

Adam stirred. "Am I needed anymore?"

"No, son, you can go." The sugar returned. "Is that alright, Ms. Costella?"

The prosecutor nodded.

Adam rose and left the courtroom. Two days later, the sentence was read.

Time's Up

"Among all kinds of killers, time is the ultimate because time kills everything."
Bhagavad Gita

"Mom. Moom."

Sidney's eyes squeezed tighter as her shoulder ebbed and flowed with movement.

"Maaaaaaaahm."

"Whaaaaaat?" Her voice creaked through unused hinges.

"I need a ride to school. I missed the bus." Annoyance and maternal duties overrode her desire to sleep. Her eyes cracked open, brows furrowed at her son, his silhouette outlined by the room's dim light. Early sunlight slithered in through closed blinds, allowing follicles of light to move over him. A ray across the chest showed he'd gotten dressed, and his backpack was thrown over his left shoulder. The light on his face made a glare on his glasses.

"I'll meet you downstairs."

"Thanks, Mom."

Sidney reached for her phone on the nightstand and unplugged it from the charger. 6:45 mocked her as she swung her legs over the side of the bed. "Start the *Keurig* for me, Ben."

"'Kay." Ben walked out the door, flipping on the light switch on his way out.

She could hear the steps groan before his sneakers resounded against the kitchen linoleum. She pushed through her closet's work shirts and dresses in favor of her *Central Park Zoo* hoodie. An anthropomorphic giraffe, lion, rhino, and tiger waved hello to Sidney before a jungle backdrop. In bolded, bubbly letters, the hoodie exclaimed *"It's a jungle out there!"* She pulled her sweatshirt over her oversized Mickey Mouse T-shirt, then her striped fleece pajama bottoms higher on her waist so they couldn't snag on her sneakers.

Static built up under her feet as she shuffled to the door. The knob zapped her as she pushed it shut.

Green Mountain's Nantucket Blend blessed the air as the *Keurig* rasped out its final drops. All lights in the upstairs hallway were off. Ben's room, the bathroom, and Michelle's room all lay in wait for

"

their next usage. She took out her hair tie, running her fingers through ebony locks. Her fingers snagged on some frizz. A stubborn flyaway refused to stay down.

"Maaaaahm! I'm gonna be *laaate!*"

"Did Michelle leave without you?"

Ben came into view as she went down the stairs. His back was leaned against the counter, his arms loosely crossed over his long-sleeved Punisher T-shirt. His hair, unlike his mother's, was managed with too much gel. It left little white specks floating in it. "Guess so. She wasn't here when I got up."

Sidney went to the *Keurig*. The East River High soccer team's travel mug steamed, beckoning for fix-ins. She opened the fridge to grab some half-and-half. "Don't you two normally leave together?"

Ben shrugged. "Sometimes. Other times she catches a ride."

"Uh-huh." Creamer splashed into the mug, boiling in translucent clouds, only to be consumed by the liquid with the swirl of a spoon. "With who?"

"You *know* who." The way his nose scrunched in distaste reminded her of herself. Ben had copied a lot from her genetic book: black hair, nose scrunches, green eyes. Michelle (God help her) took after her dad: blonde, amazing eyelashes, and tense shoulders.

"So, Jim drove her to school?" Sidney pulled open a cabinet to grab some sugar, a solitary *squeaaak* protesting the usage.

"He drove her somewhere. They left kinda early for school if you ask me."

"I didn't ask you." She scowled at her coffee and added a little less than half a spoon of sugar to her coffee. "Go start the car."

"Alright."

Sidney picked up her travel mug, tucking the closed half-and-half under her arm as she opened the fridge. When she closed it, she could see Ben standing in the middle of the hallway, staring into the living room.

The kitchen ended in an open doorway with the stairs directly outside of it to the left. The hallway stretched out to the front door, passing the living room, which shared a wall with the kitchen. She complained many times about the claustrophobic layout to Eric, but he didn't seem to mind. It reminded him of a maze, which he seemed to think was a positive.

Sidney's nose scrunched. "What are you looking at?"

"The clock stopped."

"Aw, shit." Sidney's bottom lip tucked under her teeth. "Your grandma's gonna haunt me for that one." She stood beside her son in the living room's arched doorway. The curtains on the front windows were pulled shut with the couch before them, decorative pumpkin pillows resting against either arm. Directly across from that was the TV, mounted on the back of the kitchen wall. The *La-Z-Boy* armchair separated the couch from the far wall where the grandfather clock rested. Small skylights above bathed the room in light, but this didn't penetrate the perpetual shadow that loomed around the clock. It stood motionless; the hands stopped at 3:00. Sidney's mother used to polish the clock's face constantly. The build-up of chemical cleaners cast a cataract upon the glass surface. The pendulum was pulled all the way to the left, held in place in spite of gravity. The clock had been in the family for generations and it showed. Wood splintered along its edges, the glass door required a pull. "That really sucks."

DONG!

The clock's chime had distorted at some point in her childhood. Its discordant cries never sounded the same. Sometimes it sounded slowed down, other times like an amplified squeaking door. The looming sentinel shook the air around it.

Sidney wrapped her arms around her shoulders. *Maybe it's time to put it out of its misery.*

DONG!

Ben covered his ears. The boxed in walls acted as an echo chamber. "Do you think we can fix it?"

"I hope so. I'll swing by Bill's on the way home to ask about it."

DONG!

Sidney paused in anticipation of another interruption. The grandfather clock resumed its silent vigil. "Let's go."

"Okay."

Sidney slipped on her shoes by the door as Ben took the keys from the rack. She pulled up her hood to ward off the early morning cold. The wind blew hair into her face. Crunching leaves under the tires and the carved pumpkins on porches did nothing to stave off the morning's chill. The car refused to heat up when it wasn't moving, making the red light before the school turn-in all the more frustrating. The heater puffed a sigh of relief as the car turned.

Ben ducked past his mom as she leaned over to kiss his cheek.

"Thanks, Mom. See you later."

Sidney kissed her hand, sticking it on him with all the stealth of a doting mother. "Have a good day."

"I'll try."

Sidney watched her son join the steady trickle of students who marched toward East River High. One boy clapped Ben on the shoulder and walked with him. He had on a blue East High baseball cap with a denim jacket pulled over a T-shirt. Ben's nose scrunched as he laughed at something the newcomer said.

Is that Nick Amatto or Justin Chambers?

She had more pressing things to worry about than the similarity of teenage boys, like her mother's broken clock at home, or this line, which moved with all the urgency of a grocery store customer at closing time. She brought her coffee mug to her lips, savoring the caffeine that crawled down her throat. Sidney turned on the radio. *Queen's '39* crooned as Ben started to disappear into the crowd.

That was when she saw them.

Standing by the stop sign were two boys. One had on a plaid button down, a *Misfits* T-shirt beneath. His black hair parted to the left in a cowlick. His hands were shoved into his jeans.

God, he looks so familiar.

She didn't like staring at this teen, this *boy*, but everything about him echoed familiarity.

Is he Nick? Or is that one of Michelle's exes?

Looking at this boy was easier than looking at his companion. He stood with the arrogance of a teenage boy and was the same height as his friend. The shriveled features of his face felt *off*, like someone had sanded away wrinkles from an elderly man. He looked plastic, more befitting a mall display window. Much like these mannequins, his plain black hoodie and jeans hung from him without form, only the suggestion of an outer frame.

Someone honked behind her. The car in front of her was already at the corner. She let her foot off the brake and rolled forward.

Plastic Teen pointed to Ben. Plaid Teen scrunched his nose. Ben paid them no mind. He was lost in conversation with Nick... or Justin?

The car before her turned onto the main road. Sidney followed. *I just need coffee. Coffee and sleep. I should have time for a nap before work.* Sidney brought her coffee to her lips again. Brian May's angelic voice gave way to WKPZ's very own Fitz Patrick.

"If you have plans today, you might want to move them indoors. We're expecting some nasty rain until this time tomorrow."

Sidney drowned out the radio personality with more coffee as she pulled into Lakawonna Plaza's parking lot. Darnwood Hardware occupied the left corner of the shopping center, between the Staples and Lakawonna Dollar Store. Bill Darnwood had taken over the shop once he realized the NYU animal studies program wasn't for him. The place wasn't very big, but it had a loyal clientele and supportive staff. Bill was an old friend of both herself and Eric from high school. He'd always been there, whether it was with a hand truck for moving in, or with a twelve pack of *Bud Light* on football Sundays.

A bell *tingle-linged* as Sidney entered the store. Bill was standing at the counter, cleaning it with a *Lysol* wipe. He wore a buttoned-up plaid shirt with "Darnwood Hardware" embroidered above the right breast. His brown hair parted to the right in a cowlick. The counter was U-shaped, locking the cashier behind it. The left and right arms of the countertop came up on a latch when anyone wanted to get in or out. Although there were some expensive power tools hanging on the wall behind him, the rest of the merchandise was categorized into four aisles. Each was labeled with a wooden sign hanging from the ceiling, their categories painted in black upon it. The fluorescent light above the paint aisle flickered.

Bill looked up and smiled. "Hey, Sid. Ain't this a bit early for you to be up-and-at-'em?"

Sidney shrugged. "Ben needed a ride to school."

"And you got all dressed up for the occasion, I guess?" A snort echoed against the back of his throat. He threw away the *Lysol* wipe under the counter. "What can I do for you?"

"The clock broke."

"Your mom's old one?"

"Yeah. I'm thinking it could be something with a motor, because the pendulum just stopped moving. Do those things even *have* motors?"

"Not really. They have escapements." Bill ran a hand down from his chin to his throat before scratching at his collar bone. "Did you move it?"

"Nope. It's exactly where you and Eric put it."

"Weird." Bill tapped his index finger against the counter, staring into the paint aisle for answers. "I can check in the back to see if we have the part for it. Stay put." Bill lifted the latch on the counter and brushed past his customer. He smelled like sawdust.

Sidney began to regret leaving her coffee in the car. Her head felt as if someone was squeezing the sides, waiting for it to pop. *If it's not raining, I can run out real quick and —*

Plaid Teen stood outside the window, peering through the "o" of "Darnwood." Behind him was Plastic Teen, only he didn't quite look the same. He was taller than Plaid Teen, at least by a head. His eyes looked ready to squeeze like *Play-Doh* through the sockets. His lips were too small, and his skin stretched too far across his skull, so his teeth jutted out. Some teeth covered others, some emerged in weird angles. His frame, although still as formless, was broader.

Plaid Teen placed a hand against the chipped paint on the window. Even in the rain, his cowlick refused to go down. He looked more human than he had before, less of a personification of déjà vu, more of a scared boy. His lips moved. She couldn't hear him, but she could guess the sound that came out of him. *Mom.*

"Bad news. I'll have to order it in, but..." Sidney heard Bill stop walking. "Are you okay?"

"That kid work for you?"

"What kid?"

"That boy." Sidney didn't turn to look at Bill as she addressed him. "The one outside the window." Sidney turned to face him. He was looking at her, not past her, not at the boy at the window. *How can he not see him?* "Bill, he's *right there.*" She turned to look at him again. Plaid Teen was on his knees before the Plastic Man now, holding the pencil-fingered hand as he pointed inside. Plastic Man was nodding along. His eyes never left her.

"Are you *sure* you're okay?" This time Bill came closer, placing a hand on his friend's shoulder. He squeezed. "Maybe you should go home, get some more rest. I'll call you about that part later, okay?"

The bell *tingle-linged* again as she exited again. Plastic Man and Plaid Teen were no longer outside the window. She poured the rest of her coffee onto the pavement. Even though her thoughts danced across her skull all the way home, she had to fight to keep her eyes open as soon as her head hit the pillow. She set an alarm before her consciousness retreated into the void.

Eric's kiss to her temple worked its Orphic magic, pulling her from slumber's abyss. "You're home early," she yawned.

"Yeah. And you slept right through work."

Sidney attempted to somersault from bed, but Eric's arm snaked around her waist, holding her down. She grabbed her phone from the nightstand. 5:45. The autumn darkness crept through the blinds. "I don't get it. I didn't lose track of time. I...I set an alarm. How did..."

"It's okay, babe. I called your boss; told him you weren't feeling well. He took time off your sick days or something." He filled the hole between her shoulder and neck with his head. "Bill called earlier. Said you might have a fever."

"A fever?"

"Yeah. He told me you seemed pretty out of it this morning. A fever can do that to you, y'know."

"I feel fine." Another attempt at sitting up was foiled. "Today's just been weird."

"We all have those days from time to time." Eric pressed another kiss to her temple. "Want me to cook us something? Ben needs to eat before practice anyways."

"Sure. Go ask the kids what they want. I don't really care what we have."

"Ki-*duh*. Singular. Michelle isn't home yet."

Sidney's nose scrunched. "Are you sure?"

"Ben didn't see her come in. The lights are off in her room. Unless she's playing hide and seek, she must be out with Jim."

"I guess."

"Come down when you're ready." The door was left open to the hallway. She was half blinded by the light but could still make out the outline of his shaggy hair. His footsteps *thunked* down the stairs, before muting to clicks against the linoleum.

DONG!

"The hell—"

DONG!

"Maaaaahm!"

Whatever Eric said to their son was muffled, but Ben ignored him.

"MAAAhhmm. The clock's acting *weird*."

The clock was old. It was no surprise that it stopped working and even less surprising that it would act up. As she came down the steps,

Sidney saw Eric and Ben standing in the living room's doorway, staring at the clock. The curtains were pulled open, shrouding the room in moonlight. The glass case seemed alive, its pendulum pulsing back and forth across the floor in shadow.

"Have you ever seen it move like that, Sid?" Eric's head was cocked to the side, some of his blond locks brushing against his shoulder.

"Forget that." Ben's nose scrunched. "Have you ever seen it move on the *carpet*?"

"It's just the way the light's hitting it."

"No, Dad, that's *weird*."

Sidney stood between her husband and son; eyes fixated on the grandfather clock. It read 2:00. The pendulum would pause as it got to the side, wait, then swing downward, before repeating. "Bill said it had a broken motor. Well, something along those lines anyway. It's probably just acting up."

"Yeah." Eric reached behind her to give his son a playful push. "Go stop that pendulum. We probably shouldn't let it wear itself out."

"Nuh-uh. This is weird, Dad. Isn't it weird?" Moonlight glimmered on his glasses as he looked to his mother. "It's totally weird, right, Mom?"

"I think your father is right. It'll probably break more."

"I guess so."

The pendulum hung on the right side. Ben stepped into the living room and it swung. He collapsed as the pendulum's shadow crossed his leg. The stub of his wedged ankle and foot were abandoned as he withdrew. He didn't scream, rather he whimpered and groaned, a high-pitched wheeze being all he could manage. Sidney screamed for him. As the pendulum released its hold on the left side, she darted forward. The shadow grazed her leg. A trickle of blood left a trail on the carpet. Ben, who crawled in the opposite direction, lost everything below his hips. All efforts of crawling away ceased. He fell limp against the carpet and gurgles came from his mouth, followed by involuntary hacking.

Sidney looked to her husband. Eric remained stationary in the doorway. A dark blotch ran down the front of his pants. All of his muscles were tightened. She feared that if she touched him, he would disintegrate.

She raced forward, hopping over her son's dismembered limbs. She pulled his arms. The pendulum fell from the right and sliced clear through Ben's head. His brain fell apart like sliced jello. The shadow missed her.

As the pendulum clicked into place on the left side, she abandoned the living room. "Eric—" Her voice was strangled by the tears pouring down her cheeks. "We have to call someone. The police. A… a priest." She reached for her non-existent pockets. *Fucking shit, it's still upstairs.* "Where's your phone?"

All that escaped him was a pathetic mewl. His vision was fixed past her, past reality.

"Cut the shit, Eric!" She gripped his shoulders, shaking hard. His tightened muscles rejected the movement. He began to sob. "F U C K!" This wasn't going to be of any help. She pushed past him on her way to the kitchen. His phone was resting on the counter, next to the fridge. His lock screen *was* a photo of the four of them on vacation, but Michelle and Ben were no longer there. Eric had his arm around air. Sidney looked to be hugging herself.

She dialed 911.

No dial tone, no static. Nothing.

Sidney slammed the red button with her index finger and dialed again.

Deafening silence.

She hung up, this time slamming the face of the phone down onto the counter over and over. Invisible spiders spun webs on the glass. *My phone's upstairs. I can try that.* Sidney turned to rush to the stairs.

The Plastic Man stood before the front door. Eric acted as a buffer between them. The stranger's "normal" clothes were now gone. He now wore a black cloak that made his pale skin blinding. Wrinkles reclaimed his face, and his teeth grew over his lips. His shriveled eyes were gone, leaving behind only black sockets. He bit down in a grin, before clicking his tongue against the front of his mouth. *tick.*

"Who—who are you?"

His tongue clicked against the back of his mouth. *tock.* "Inevitability."

"I- I don't—"

"You do not need to. Your time has come to an end." When the Plastic Man spoke, layers of skin could be seen inside his mouth, flopping with his jaw-like jowls.

tick.

"Eric." Sidney reached toward her husband, who promptly collapsed, folding backwards on himself. His mouth was wide open, his skin pruned and gray. Black sludge poured from his eyes.

tock.

She couldn't scream. Her throat felt stuffed with cotton. She wanted to lunge, to fight her way past the Plastic Man, but she couldn't. He was inevitable. Her hands gripped one another and pulled into her chest. Tears only came when she tried to talk. The salt felt bitter on her tongue. "What did you do to him?"

"Time is over. It must begin anew."

"What does that mean?"

Tick tock. "This Time is no longer needed. Randy has returned to his own Time."

"Randy?"

He smiled. The Plastic Man's teeth stabbed into his bottom lip, puncturing it, a red tear falling down to his chin. "Yes. Your son."

My son. Sidney's gaze flashed over to the living room. Ben laid where she'd left him, brains, blood, and clear ooze poured from the open cornucopia. The pendulum's shadow passed over him again and again.

DONG!

Plaid Teen invaded her thoughts. His scrunched-up nose as he pointed to Ben. His quivering lip as he had pressed his hand to the glass and whispered into the void. *"Mom."*

"It's time for a reunion."

"No!" Sidney bolted up the stairs. She didn't hear his steps following her. Only the ever faster *ticktockticktock.*

The lights were on in Michelle's room.

When did she get home? I need to help her. I need to help my baby.

She threw open the door and slammed it shut behind her.

ticktockticktocktic.

The Plastic Man didn't bother with the handle.

Michelle lay on the bed. Her pink sweater was torn open, revealing her bra underneath. Its once white lace was polluted by the red lake residing between her breasts. Her head was pointed to the ceiling, her arms sprawled over the sides in a mock *pieta.* Melody's face was withered like Eric's, black sludge from her eyes trickling down onto seashell bed sheets.

ticktocktick

How long has she been here?

Sidney wanted to cradle her, cup her cheeks in her hands, wail into nothingness. She couldn't.

ticktocktickticktocktickticktock

Sidney ran to the window and pulled back the curtain.

Outside was nothing. White expanses dominated everything.

tick.

Only a few outlines smattered about were left: an outline of a tree there, the scribble of a house here.

tock.

"Time is over."

Sidney felt a hand on her shoulder.

"Time to be with your *real* family."

"I have my own family."

"You did." *tick tock.* "But now Time is up."

A Cannibal's Guide to A Cheap Meal

This story was originally published in The Normal Review's Spring 2019 edition.

Cannibalism isn't illegal, in case you were wondering. Really. Look it up. Cannibalism is legal, but the means of getting this *spécialité* tends to be where people get hung up. Murder, abuse of a dead human body, organ trafficking, the list goes on. You get the picture: all of these things are *very* illegal, which is why you have to be smart. I have a connection. In fact, I'm looking forward to seeing her today.

Our usual meeting spot is the Oakridge Diner. It's a mom-and-pop sort of place, with rustic charm and rustic waitresses. The place brings that good ol' small town atmosphere that comes with a sarcastic waitress and mediocre service. Some may say that it's worth the couple extra bucks to go to Shelly's Diner up the road, but I think this diner has far better hash browns. I sit alone at my usual booth by the window as I wait for my supplier. I wrap both my hands around the generic white ceramic mug as I enjoy the warm sensation that comes from this. Not because it's cold outside, mind you, it's July — I just think the feeling is nice and soothing.

As I lean back against the hard, plastic booth, I tune out the waitresses gossiping at the 50's style counter in favor of looking out to the street through the smudged window. A young family is window-shopping. The dad is pushing a stroller with a little tyke in it, chatting happily away with the mom about God-knows-what. Thomas, the decrepit and handsy owner of Cooper's Pub, sets out a sign out front by the corner. It proudly announces that tonight is "Ladies Night." All women drink for half off, if they're willing to brave the lewd comments thrown their way.

"You're early," a voice like freshly squeezed lemons chides me. I look up to see the bitter, ravenesque beauty known as Maria. She has long black hair that cascades over her shoulders in smooth waves. Maria's wearing a light green sweater that few others could pull off with dark jeans to complement it. Her olive skin is tanned due to her inclination towards long, lazy days at the beach. Maria's brown eyes would be beautiful if they weren't always so cold. Looking into them is like looking into those Greek sculptures of goddesses, although even those have more emotion carved into them. Her sweet voice is always bitter when she talks to me. My assumption has always been that it's because she finds me repugnant. That's what she tells me anyway.

"You know what they say." I smile. "The early bird gets the worm."

"Yeah, well, I've got your worm for you." As Maria sits, she pulls out her Galaxy S9+ and holds it out to me. As I take it, we both notice that my hand is shaking. She attributes it to excitement and becomes more disgusted than before. I ignore it, because this has been happening for about a week now. I chalk it up to nerves.

I examine the picture of the man presented to me and become disappointed. He's muscular, which means his meat will be tough. At least he looks healthy. It would be worse if I couldn't salvage any of it. My last meal happened to come from a smoker. Touching a tar-riddled lung is like touching the rocks covered in slime at a riverbed. The tough meat of this gym-junkie would be a dream in comparison. I scroll to the second photo, a screenshot of her notes. It has the time and place that I'll be meeting Maria's hitman: two am at the usual abandoned warehouse. Cliché, but perfect for this kind of trade-off. Also included is the name of the poor sap who'll become dinner: Richard Simpkins. I never cared much for this type of information, but I don't have the heart or the balls to tell Maria that.

"What'd he do to deserve your wrath?"

Maria shrugged. "I'm sick of him. I gave him a loan and he keeps skipping payments. Don is dealing with him tonight."

I'd be afraid of Maria if I didn't know I was useful to her. She talks about people the way my Aunt Franca talks about the cashier who wouldn't refill her coupon.

I return her phone to her before I take a sip of my stale, lukewarm coffee. I chide myself for not drinking it while it was stale, hot coffee. Debbie, the red-haired waitress, never makes a good batch. Flo, the old sweetheart who works out of boredom in retirement, makes the best. I should've known better to meet Maria on one of

Flo's days off. The liquid sloshes about in the cup as my shaking hand holds it to my lips. This prompts a look from Maria that I haven't seen before. If I didn't know any better, I might mistake it for pity.

"What's wrong with you?"

"Sorry?"

Maria gestures vaguely in my general direction. "You can't keep your hand steady."

Something about the fact that she at least half cares makes me smile. "Its been doing that for a week or so. I hardly notice it anymore."

"Maybe being a human garbage disposal is catching up to you."

I doubt it. I've been doing this for four years, so I know all the tricks. Human meat is high in calories, so I'm careful to balance human and "normal" meats. "Maybe." I sip my coffee once again, and the ceramic hits my teeth because of my unsteadiness. "You want to stick around?"

"Never."

"Why not?"

Maria proceeds to slide out of my booth. "'Cause you disgust me."

There's the Maria I know and love. This no longer hurts my feelings, as I'm used to it, but my smile fades away. "You can't think I'm that bad."

"Oh?"

"You're the one that keeps calling me back here."

She glares at me. "Just don't keep Don waiting." Maria ignores my attempt to wave goodbye as she slips out onto the street.

***

I stand over what was once Richard Simpkins as Don idly guards the door. The beloved hitman reminds me of a shaved gorilla. He certainly has the flat face and bulging muscles of one. His forehead is hidden under a black beanie. A matching black t-shirt hugs his inhumanly pale skin. His deep-set eyes are a trademark of his brutal nature.

"You really butchered his throat, hm? Not much to work with."

Don grunts, which makes me afraid to speak to him again. I don't need his help, anyway. I've come prepared. I've brought my backpack of tools, which contains knives, scalpels, and trash bags. I also have my two coolers, the ones that you see at any barbecue: the blue plastic ones that have white lids. These coolers, much like their cousins at the barbecue, are filled with ice.

Now, it's hard to go about this when you think of the meat as a person. I've learned to view people as one views cows: they can be nice and cute while also serving as a great meal. It's never fun to see the animal your meat comes from, even if you didn't kill it yourself. You grow thicker skin as time goes on. By my third or fourth harvest I no longer felt bothered, as the labor is worth the result.

I start with the meat. I peel and carve away the more appealing bits, which I place into the first cooler. The scraps and inedible portions get placed off to the side for later disposal. Now, I'm no specialist, but I have mastered some skills over the years. I can now get the meat out without hacking it to shreds. The only problem is that all of this work is incredibly time-consuming and there's *a lot* of meat. Once this is complete, I have one cooler filled, and I'm ready to move on to the organs. I'm a liver fanatic. I know, it's not a popular item, but trust me. When you cook it just right, it really pops. I also enjoy the stomach prepared as a haggis. Once again, not very popular, but you don't become a cannibal when you have renowned eating habits. I take other organs too, such as the heart, brain, lungs, tongue — the list goes on.

"This will keep me content for quite a while," I comment to Don as I pack away what remains of the carcass into the trash bags. "Thank you again."

"Whatever, you sick fuck."

I feign a wounded look. "Aw, Don, how could you? I'm not all that bad. After all, *I'm* not the one that killed him." Don didn't appreciate my quip. Don never appreciates my quips. Maria should really hire a hitman with a sense of humor. I leave the warehouse to avoid becoming his next victim. My coolers rattle as my legs wobble underneath me, which I attribute to my fear of the meatball I'm leaving behind. The scariest part of my journey has yet to come: the drive home.

Butchery has the unpleasant side effect of making you smell like death. The entire ride tends to consist of praying no one sees me and attempting to ignore the smell. A chopped-up human body reeks, but the result is worth putting up with the stench. Besides, if you have strong enough *Febreeze* vent clips, you hardly notice it. A perk of having these meetings in the wee hours of the night is that hardly any people are out and about. It only takes one person to see you for the whole business to go down the drain. Once, a cop car followed behind me for a few miles, and I was half tempted to just pull over and confess. Eventually, he pulled into a *7-Eleven* and my anxieties were gone.

I'm lucky enough to get home without any sign of the police to drive me to panic. My coolers rest on the tile floor of my kitchen with the lids open as I prep the meat into their own plastic storage containers. My cat, Lee, sniffs at the contents of my tubs until I shoo him away. It's not until I pack away the very last item that I realize I'm starving. I open the fridge and stare blankly into it until something appeals to me. I ended up choosing the tub marked "Brains" in blue *Sharpie* marker. I've had this recipe for maple sausage and eggs I've been dying to try, and little brain patties should work wonderfully. The kitchen fills with a delightful aroma as I cook my meal on the stove.

The smell reminds me of when I decided to try out this cannibalism shtick. I was at Wellman's, the local grocery store, buying my dinner for the week. A coworker had recommended organic meats, which I soon found out were ridiculously overpriced. If you think about it, everything aside from junk food is expensive. I grumbled over this concept until I got to the register. I ignored the old woman yelling at the underpaid cashier as I looked over the magazine rack. One particularly interesting cover advertised the story of a man from Germany who'd looked for someone on the Internet to volunteer to be a willing meal. Obviously, someone died in the process, but the culprit was only charged for murder, sweeping his choice of delicacy under the proverbial carpet. I thought that might be an interesting way to save money. I don't have to pay anything for most of my meat now. I do my job for Maria *pro bono* to help her get rid of her victims. Win-win.

You might think this is a bit weird, but I could be doing *much* worse. I could've been killing these people myself, but I'm not heartless.

My meal finishes with my reverie. I take it to the head of my dining room table with a tall glass of orange juice. Before I can take my first bite, my swan song sounds. The three loud bangs of a fist against my door could have very well been death's bell sounding off. I look down and notice that my clothes are splattered with blood from my meal prep. Guests tend to disapprove highly of such things. Perhaps I can explain it away. Hopefully I can explain it away. As I attempt to stand, I notice something frightening. I can't. Even as I push my trembling hands against the table to hoist myself up, my legs refuse to cooperate and buckle under me.

That's when the policemen kick down my door. All of them have their guns trained on me. All of them look angry. "Get on your knees and place your hands behind your head!" My response to this surprised even myself.

I laugh.

I laugh a boisterous, crazed, uncontrollable laugh. I can't help it. I can't stop. I'm terrified, yet the laughter will not cease.

My last memory is of the police throwing me to the ground.

***

I wake up in a hospital room. Everything around me is bright white. As I try to push myself up, I notice that I'm handcuffed to the bed rail. Great. A whiteboard is on the wall in front of me with a clipboard to the side of it. My name is written on it, along with the names of my doctor and nurse. The handwriting is not dissimilar to that of the bubbly lettering of a teenage girl.

I hear a gentle knock on the door before a woman enters. She has her blond hair tied back in a tight bun. She is wearing the typical doctor's get up—white coat, stethoscope, the works. The fact that she's my doctor is confirmed by the name on her nametag, Susan Walters, matching that on the whiteboard.

"How long was I out?"

"A few hours."

"I see."

Doctor Walters approaches my bed, resting a carefully manicured hand next to my shackles. "I have a question for you, and you need to answer honestly."

"I'll do my best to, sure."

"Have you ever eaten human brains before?"

I hesitate but find no reason to lie to the doctor. The police would've told her what they found me eating. At least, I assume they would.

"It's not my favorite, but I don't like to waste anything."

Doctor Walters nods as she grabs the clipboard from the wall. "But you have eaten it more than once?"

"Yes. I can't give you an exact number, but over the years I've had my share. Why?"

"Thought as much. I just needed to be sure before I diagnosed you." The doctor lifts a page from the clipboard before letting it fall, allowing for her attention to return to me. "You have kuru."

"What is that?"

"A rare neurodegenerative disorder that comes from eating human brains," the doctor explains. I suddenly miss the sarcasm and bitterness of Maria—at least there's some feeling behind it. "From what we can gather, you seem to be at stage two." I must look confused, because she adds, "In other words, you suffer from severe shaking, emotional instability, and sporadic laughter. Also, you won't be able to walk without support anymore."

"Am I going to be okay?"

Dr. Walters stirs, though she maintains the stoic face of someone who often has to deliver bad news. "We'll do everything in our power to make sure you're comfortable. Unfortunately, kuru is fatal. You will—"

The doctor is interrupted by my unbridled laughter. I laugh so hard that the bed begins to shake as violently as I do.

Deck the Halls

This short story was originally published in The Normal Review's Fall 2020 edition.

The wooden double panel door splintered as the crowbar was inserted into the side opposite its hinges. Little strength was required in order to force the lock, as it hadn't been changed since the 70's. The door handle would wriggle in its place when turned, almost as if it could be screwed out. The once polished wood was faded and adorned with scars. Some of these were initials, others were various profanities.

Al Harvey kicked the door in after one last push with the crowbar. The door huddled against the wall in order to escape the intruder's wrath. Harvey dropped his crowbar to the concrete step below him, whose clatter was muffled by the light dusting of snow below his feet. Al had little concern for anyone seeing him enter on camera or otherwise. The brick wall of the alleyway next to him was his only witness since the Church of Saint Nicholas was devoid of security cameras. All the church had was Father Abraham and the will of God to defend it—whatever the fuck that meant. Al could have sworn that the place was giftwrapped for him. If the will of God was to keep this church safe, then why wouldn't he divinely inspire Abraham to get *Ring* or some other security system? If anything, he was helping the old fart by teaching him how the world works.

Al cut through the darkness, striding towards the other side of the room. The only light was supplied from the skylight above, which was slowly being buried in a shallow layer of snow, and the advent wreath. He cast his gaze over the congregation of pews to the altar. Jesus hung his head above them, looking down at the intruder below.

"Careful, Hey-soos. Stayin' quiet when there's a crime makes ya guilty by association," Al warned.

Jesus maintained his silent vigil over the pews.

Harvey swung open the door that led down a corridor. It was a stark contrast to the warm aura the church exuded. The walls were stark white, only interrupted by a framed picture of St. Nicholas. The white and blue tiles led Al down the hallway toward his destination. The saint smiled at the man as he passed. The saint of giving, as well as repentant thieves, could only extend his influence as far as the frame before him. He brought no obstacle against Harvey.

Al pushed the door marked *Office* open. On the inside, to the left of the door, was a drop-box to the toy drive. A brown teddy bear with a Santa hat judged Al as he moved to the desk across from it. The burglar lifted the lockbox, which contained donations to both the church and poor, from its place on the desk. As he turned on his heel to leave, he was met by Father Abraham, who now stood in the doorway. Al hardly recognized him in his striped pajama bottoms and *Simpsons* T-shirt.

"Out of the way, Father."

Father Abraham took a cautious step forward. The eyes beyond the bags of wrinkles seemed hurt. "On Christmas Eve? My son—"

"I'm not your fucking son." As Al spoke, he raised his shirt to show the gun tucked into his pants. "Move."

The old man hung his head. "On this holiest of days, where it is our duty to give to those less fortunate, I can't let you steal from them."

Al's cold gray eyes stared into those of the Father before he sprung forward. He grabbed the priest by the shirt and cast him against the toy-bin. There was a sickening crack. Blood started to pool on the top of his shirt and dripped from his ear. As the bear hit the ground, it began to sing Deck the Halls. He poked the priest and his head lulled to the side.

"Fa-la-la-la-laaa la-la-la-lah," the bear sang.

Al clutched the lockbox in his fist as he left the room. The door slamming cut the bear off mid song. He strode down the hallway and into the church. Jesus averted his gaze from the criminal. The nave was darker now that the snow completely covered the skylight above. Harvey was quick to leave the building, entering into the alleyway from whence he had come. A woman and her daughter walked past the mouth of the alley. Al was invisible to them, or so it seemed, as neither of them looked his way.

"Deck the halls with boughs of holly," the child sang as she skipped ahead of her mother.

Al waited for the pair to pass before he went back onto the sidewalk. He started walking west, passing the church on his left. A man passed by the grand church steps, his face buried in his phone. His eyes scanned over a message he had received, and he groaned.

"'Tis the season to be jolly," the man muttered.

Al stopped in his tracks, and watched the stranger as he passed. It was not long before he shook his head. He walked forward to the corner of Deacon and Main. A Honda pulled up to the stop sign. Another car's tires swerved on ice as it turned the corner, nearly hitting the Honda. The offended car honked its horn.

"Fa-la-la-la-laaa la-la-la-lah," the car horn yelled.

"What the fuck..."

He was hearing things. He had to be hearing things. He was just feeling guilty about offing the old man. That was all and nothing more. An old woman with curled white hair stood next to him. She held a bag with a yorkie in it. The dog's small eyes looked up to him as she whimpered in tune. Al ignored the dog, and tapped the woman on the shoulder. "Did ya see that car? That coulda been some wreck, amirite?"

"See the blazing Yule before us," she responded softly.

His face fell. The old woman hobbled across the street, blissfully unaware of what she had just said. Al stayed still as a group of college kids came towards him. One of the boys in a university sweatshirt playfully shoved a friend.

"Strike the harp and join the chorus," said the young man in the sweatshirt.

"Fa-la-la-la-laaa la-la-la-lah," the other grumbled.

Al ran forward, intent on leaving the church far behind him. Instead of dissipating, the song got louder. If there were no people near him, then the song would come from a radio, or from the clicking of a turn signal.

"Sing we joyous all together..."

"Troll the ancient Yuletide carol..."

"While I tell of Yuletide treasure..."

"While I tell of Yuletide treasure..."

"WHILE I TELL OF YULETIDE TREASURE."

Al screamed and rushed into the nearest alleyway. He slid his back down against a wall. The snow seeped in through his jeans and caused him to shiver, but he didn't care. He kept his lockbox in his lap as he pulled his knees upwards. Harvey rested his head against his knees and covered his ears with his hands.

It had to stop.

It *had* to stop.

"You look like you're yearning for peace," a soft voice commented.

Al looked up to see Father Abraham standing before him. He was now adorned in his white vestment, a purple scarf hanging over his shoulders. He seemed to have washed off the blood from himself, as there was no trace of it. Everything was quiet.

"Father, you've got to stop this. I can't fucking take it," the burglar begged. He moved from his fetal position to his knees at Abraham's feet. "Please, Father."

The priest smiled down at the man. "There's only one way for this to end, my son."

The money.

The box had fallen off of his lap and into the snow as he moved to his knees. He lifted it up, and thrust it towards the old man. "Take it. It's all yours."

The priest took the box from his hands before vanishing.

Strike the harp and join the chorus.

No.

Strike the harp and join THE CHORUS.

No, God, please, no.

STRIKE THE HARP AND JOIN THE CHORUS.

STRIKE THE HARP AND JOIN THE CHORUS.

Al reached into his belt, and pulled out his gun. Gray matter splattered against the wall as Al's soul left the old world passing.

Decaytion

"Seriously, take it." Diane swatted the air in assault of a non-existent fly with a gift certificate. "You'd be doing me a favor."

Bea tugged her plaid blanket around her shoulders. "This doesn't sound like a favor."

"Look, I got this from Roman." Diane continued her flaunting inches from her sister's face. "I can't give that prick the satisfaction of using it."

"That petty logic doesn't add up. I mean, wouldn't it make *more* sense for you to burn it or something?"

"Look." Diane reached across the counter to hold Bea's hand. "You deserve this, okay? This writing thing, it's getting to you, hun. You need some space from it, some time to breathe."

Bea looked down at their hands. Diane's neon green gel extensions radiated off of her nail beds and likely blinded the closest airline pilot. "I dunno, Dee. Spas aren't really my thing."

"Oh, *please*. Massages are everyone's thing." She squeezed the other's hand. "Do it for me, huh? I worry about you."

Bea relented. Both the gift certificate (good for one full-service trip) and Dee's blanket accompanied her on the drive home. She sat in her driveway for a while, swirling patterns on the back of her hand with her thumb. The gift emanated the foreboding allure of freedom: no commitments, no work. A novel was a masochistic mistress. It required following numerous threads with precision and orchestrating moving parts. Attention to detail, focus, dedication were all required for this task. All of this was without gratitude or guarantee of success, and all of these would be neglected if work was abandoned for a getaway. Dissociative fugues and random fits of crying, however, were also hindering productivity.

"Fine," Bea grumbled. "You win."

The gift certificate crinkled triumphantly under her grip as she escorted it inside. As soon as she stepped in the front door, Sugar squealed from across the lobby. Her front paws gripped the bars of her home as her teeth pulled at the cage door. "Hi, squeaky girl." Bea shuffled to the counter and placed down her gift. The living room and kitchen collided and culminated in a brackish living space.

Everything about the decor screamed "I live alone." All thought that may have been put toward decoration was saved for managing organized chaos. No appliance nor furniture had been revamped since Bea moved in, and she liked it that way. The only active example of life was Sugar's corner. Hay and pellets were piled next to the guinea pig's McMansion. Much like her owner, and unlike the rest of her species, Sugar seemed to do better solo, so she was spoiled accordingly.

Bea knelt by the cage and unlatched the door. "Wanna help your mama plan to leave you for a day?" The Abyssinian was pleased to receive scritches behind her ears, as evidenced by a low coo, but she forced her mother's hand to chase her in circles before consenting to be held. The pair nestled on the couch as the owner pulled up the spa on her phone.

Swansong Spa: Relax. Renew. Revive.

Bea scrolled through pictures of people in dimly lit rooms in white, embroidered robes. One woman partook in the stereotypical facial; cream on face, cucumbers on the eyes, cares lost in caresses. Another showed two men, face down, holding hands as they received a massage from women in black tunics and white slacks. The facility itself was not above cliché. Polished granite tiles, marble, and hardwood floors (all of which were likely to reek of lavender incense) made up the spa interior. The most jarring part of the website was the prices. It was guaranteed to revive panic after a soothing session. She booked a treatment before she could reconsider.

Her phone gave a staccato buzz in her pocket as she put Sugar back in her cage. A text from a five-digit number awaited her on the home screen.

Thank you for booking with us at Swansong Spa! We look forward to servicing you. Please fill out our brief questionnaire to ensure the highest quality service.

The survey asked the following:

Have you been to one of our locations before?

What is the reason for your visit?

Are you in any pain?

Are you allergic to any oils?

What pressure do you prefer for your massage?

Who referred you?

Is there anything we can do to make your experience memorable?

When Bea finished, a screen with a smiley face popped up to thank her for her time.

***

Swansong Spa interrupted the forest. The woods never disbanded, instead they grew around the facility like an extension of it. A swan-shaped sign pointed Bea to a packed parking lot. Her *I arrived safe! How is my girl?* text pretended to send for a minute before deciding that service was unavailable. The outside of the spa left the impression of a rustic log cabin as opposed to the pristine sanctum portrayed online.

A doorman popped out of the entrance to hold the door for the approaching guest. He wore a white tunic with a black swan embroidered on the right breast and black slacks. White hair was cut close, and he wore a thick mustache that seemed to move with his smile. "Welcome to Swansong, Ms."

Bea paused outside the doorway before stepping around the man into the spa. "Thanks."

"Do you have bags in your car?"

"No, I don't."

His smile refused to falter. "Very well. Please go to see the reception desk then. They will get you settled in."

"Great. Thanks again."

"Of course, Ms. May you leave here a better you."

Bea found herself nodding as she moved across the dimly lit room. Her footfall echoed throughout the lobby. The reception desk was in front of a wall fountain with the facility's logo etched in it. A massive white slab of marble served as the barrier between desk and guest.

A blonde woman with a tight bun at the top of her head beamed up at her. Just like the doorman, she sported a white tunic. "Welcome to Swansong Spa! Could I help you check in today?"

"Yeah, sure." Bea rummaged in her jeans pocket for the gift certificate. "It should be under Bea."

"Ah yes! Our new guest." The receptionist clapped her hands together. "On behalf of our staff, allow me to be the first to extend a warm welcome."

"Oh." Bea shifted from one foot to the next. "Thanks."

"The pleasure is ours, Bea! We hope to see more of you in the future."

The earnestness of the other woman's tone almost made Bea feel guilty sliding the gift certificate across the counter. "We'll see. I really only got to come here because of my sister."

The receptionist's demeanor remained buoyant. "Very understandable. Most of our clients feel the same way in the beginning, and yet, after their services, they tend to see us as a worthy investment."

Bea shifted once more. "Yeah. We'll see."

"We sure will. Please, feel free to take a seat. Your massage therapist will be with you momentarily. May you leave here a better you!"

Bea retreated from the desk and into the larger lobby. Most of the lighting came from candles along wooden walls. White leather sofas were scattered about the room with an excess of black pillows on them. She chose an empty one and sunk into it. Another attempt to contact her sister about her arrival was made in vain, so she took a look around the room. A couple sat on a couch near the far wall, talking in a whisper. Another older woman sat close by and played *Candy Crush* at full volume.

A frosted glass door next to reception opened up, and a woman slipped into the room. She was older, although she tried to cover it with makeup, and the ends of her hair were dyed pink. Her tunic was black with a white swan, and her slacks were white. "Bea?"

"That's me." Bea rose from the couch, slipping her phone back into her hoodie pocket.

The masseuse rushed over. "My name's Linda. I'll be taking care of you today." She offered a tight-lipped smile to her client before ushering her toward the door. Herb-scented oil wafted to Bea as her massage therapist moved. "Is this your first spa visit, Bea?"

"In general? Yeah. I did get a *Massage Envy* gift card for Christmas one year though."

Linda nodded. "Well, we're happy you chose Swansong for your first experience."

"Yeah, thanks."

Linda gave another close-mouthed smile as she held the door for her client. "Of course."

The spa looked much like it did online. Wooden floors and marble tiled walls were intermittently broken up by serene pictures and unnumbered doorways. The light, much like in the lobby, came from candles along the wall, however, they were more spaced out. The hallways were thin and winding, yet Linda navigated them with ease. Then, seemingly at random, she stopped abruptly to open a door for her client. "Before we begin, we are going to have a quick intake."

Bea stepped into the room. Inside was a bed with tan covers, a mini-fridge on the counter, and come cabinets above it. Whales sang from some unknown source in the room. She crossed her arms loosely over her chest. "Okay, sure."

"Great." Linda clasped her hands before her as she stood in the doorway. "It said in your file you're here for a stress detox?"

Bea nodded. "Yeah, my sister gifted it to me."

"That's nice. What has you bummed out? Job? Boyfriend or girlfriend? Life?"

"Well, I'm writing—"

"So you need extra attention to your hands and shoulders?"

"...Sure." Bea rubbed her hands together. "But, really, it's just everything is coming all at once. The job's demanding, bills are due, publishers are publishers."

"I getcha." Linda flashed one of her now trademarked smiles. "And you said you like firm pressure?"

"Uh-huh."

"And no allergies to any oils that you know of?"

"Nope."

"Good, good. And how long have you been experiencing self-hatred?"

Bea blinked, but the scene before her remained unchanged. Linda still stood with her hands clasped, the sound of whales singing still droned in the background, and the question still lingered in the air. "Excuse me?"

"I asked if you've been experiencing any pain lately?"

"Oh. No, not really." Bea wrung her hands again. "Do you actually have a bathroom I can use?"

"Oh! Of course. Restrooms are at the end of the hall to the right."

"Great, thanks."

"Not a problem." Linda stepped out of the doorway to allow her client to pass. "When you get back, just undress and lie under the covers face down. I'll be sure to knock before I come in, okay?"

Bea nodded as she moved past her masseuse. The trip to the bathroom was made without trouble navigating. The sink was swan shaped, with the neck serving as the fount, and the wings serving as the handles. A picture of rocks towered in a stream was hung on the center of the wall. She pulled the right wing and splashed cool water onto her face. *You're hearing shit. You need this. You deserve this. Don't ruin it for yourself.* Bea grabbed a *Kleenex* hand towel to dry her face before she stepped back into the hallway. Linda was nowhere in sight and all of the doors were closed once more. "Well, shit." Bea passed four doors, then five, and silently cursed herself for not paying more attention. Each seemed copy-and-pasted from the same source.

I guess it can't hurt to guess. She picked the nearest door and pulled it open.

The first thing she saw were the metal clamps. They rose from the side of the table, reaching over the client, then down to his back. The man's skin was peeled down the middle and folded to the bedside with the clamps holding it in place. The massage therapist kneaded into the muscle, staining her arms and hands red. The blood squelched beneath the movement, pouring over the client's sides and pooling on the floor.

Bea never felt herself let go of the knob. She didn't hear her own screams or notice when she collapsed. Reality crashed back down upon her when Linda placed her hand on her shoulder. She now noticed a few massage therapists poking their heads out of their rooms. Confused murmurs from concerned clients drowned out the atmospheric music that came from the room across from them.

"Are you alright?" Linda gently squeezed Bea's shoulder.

"Is that guy alright? His back... It was... He was..." She trailed off and simply pointed to the open doorway before her.

Linda pursed her lips and looked toward the open door. "Jamie, how's Mr. Wincroft?"

"A bit worried, but otherwise fine." Jamie stepped to the side of the bed, revealing her client. He was sitting up on his cot, blanket over his lap, skin in one piece. "Is your client okay, Lin?"

"But, but—he was... I saw..."

"Hun." Linda returned her attention to Bea. "I think your stress is really getting to you. Does this happen a lot?"

The writer shook her head.

"I think you need an upgrade. You should really see Sarah before our massage, she's our acupuncture specialist. She'll do wonders for you."

"Isn't acupuncture for pain management?"

"Traditionally, yes. I don't know how it works really, but I know it has to do with the nervous system, so it can help with the brain. Sarah could probably explain it better. Lots of people come here for her to help with their anxiety."

Bea clutched her hands together. "I don't know if I can afford an add-on like that."

Linda's closed smile returned. "Don't worry about that. It's complimentary. I feel responsible, you know, I really should have guided you back."

Bea nodded slowly, still maintaining her grip.

"'Atta girl. Come on, let me bring you back to your room." The massage therapist offered her client a hand, which she took. Their room was only two down from the one Bea barged into. Linda once again held the door for her client. "You're going to do pretty much the same thing I said before, except you are going to be face-*up*, okay?"

"Okay."

"I'll see you afterwards." Linda clicked the door back into place, leaving Bea alone with the whale sounds. She took in deep swallows of air before undressing. All but her underwear was then folded and stacked neatly on the counter. The cot was heated, as were the blankets. Bea pulled them up to her chin before she closed her eyes. *Breathe. You need this. You deserve this. Everything is going to be okay.*

The tapping at the door did not register with her until it creaked open. She turned her head to see a woman with long, black hair draped over her shoulders. The acupuncturist moved it aside with a flourish, revealing her white embroidered swan. "Lin tells me you want some acupuncture?"

"She recommended it," Bea corrected. "I've never had it before. I don't really like needles."

Sarah's smile dripped from her lips like honey. As she got closer to the bed, Bea could make out wrinkles around her mouth. "You'll hardly feel anything, sweetie, but if it helps, you can close your eyes."

"I think I'll take you up on that."

Even as Bea complied, she could hear Sarah buzzing around the room. "Let me tell you what's going to happen. That makes it less scary, doesn't it?"

The client nodded.

"So for stress, we're going to be focusing on your DU-20, M-HN-3, GB-21, REN 17, HT-7, SP-6, and LR-4. Wait—Lin told me you write. I'll add on the PC-6, LI-4, and TB-3, just for giggles."

"I have no idea what any of that means, but okay."

"Oh, all that is just mumbo-jumbo for points on your body. Really, I just said it aloud so I didn't forget. I just said we are working on your hands, wrists, feet, ankles, sternum, shoulders, and head."

"That sounds like a lot."

"Believe me, you'll feel so much better afterwards. Trust the process."

Bea forced out an exhale.

"Your hand, sweetie."

"Oh, sorry." Bea removed her arm from under the blanket, careful to not disturb the rest of it. "Ready when you are, I guess."

"That's the spirit." All footfall ceased. Bea could feel Sarah's presence at her side— not in the *Star Wars* way, but in the hollow feeling you get when someone enters your room as you nap, only Sarah's presence hardly felt empty. Cold filled the void inside of her and rose up to her throat, to her head, to the end of every hair on her body.

Bea opened her eyes just as Sarah brought down the metal stake. Pain refused to register, even when she stared at the object protruding from her hand. "What the… wh… what?"

Sarah's lips oozed once more. "Just relax, Bea. It's all a part of the process." The acupuncturist reached out a hand that was immediately shuddered off. "Please, hold still."

Bea rolled off the bed in a cocoon of sheets as the next spike was driven toward her wrist. She fumbled to her feet, abandoning the blanket on the floor. Her uninjured hand moved to the metal and tore it free. The blood brought pain along with it as it pooled in her hand, seeped through her fingers, dripped on her bare legs.

"There's a saying in acupuncture that tells us blood allows a fresh breeze to enter the body. It's a renewal." Sarah took a step toward her client but stopped when Bea held up her stake. "How do you expect us to help you if you won't renew? You need to trust us, trust the process if you truly want to be healed."

"Fuck the process," Bea spat. "And fuck you, too." Sarah made no effort to stop her as she pushed out the door. She had half been expecting Linda and a gaggle of spa workers to capture her and usher

her back to her table, but she was alone. She screamed, only this time it seemed that she was the only one to hear it. No concerned workers looked into the hall, no customers mumbled from open doorways. It was just her, naked and bleeding in the hall. Bea's grip on the metal spike remained tight in spite of the blood that gushed from her palm. *Bitch had to stab my dominant hand, didn't she?*

Blood drizzled on the tile floor as she darted through labyrinthine halls. It wasn't a far walk from reception, and yet she found herself ever deeper in the spa. The same doorways seemed to loop with each turn she took. Bea gave up screaming. Either the walls were soundproof, or no one cared enough to check on her.

"This isn't helping, this isn't helping," she muttered to herself. She needed help, and it was looking more like her only resource would be someone familiar with the facility. *They can't all be fucking crazy, right?* Bea picked a door at random and threw it open. "Help! Hel…"

An aesthetician looked up from his client. The man in the chair had cucumbers on his eyes and foam on his face. It was white with swirls of deep red and a lighter pink. A glob dropped to the floor as he turned to look at the intruder. His face was on his chest.

"Oh, dear, you're bleeding." The aesthetician wiped his stained hands on a towel and took a cautious step forward. "Where's your caretaker? You need to get back to them before —"

"Oh *fuck* this." She bolted from the room, ignoring whatever the man called after her. *I gotta get home, I gotta get home, I gotta —*

Her mantra was interrupted when she slammed into a person after turning a corner. She looked up to see a man in a black t-shirt and jeans peering down at her. It was only now, when help seemed to be near, that Bea became self-conscious. She crossed one arm over her chest as she reached for the stranger with the other. "Please, you've got to help me. They —"

"Good work, Marcel!" Linda slipped out from behind the man. "You had us worried. I mean, look at your poor hand."

"Please, please, I just want to go home."

"How could we send you home like that? You're bleeding." Linda smiled, revealing teeth like arrow heads. "Look, hun, all this is a part of the process."

"I don't want to be a part of the process anymore," Bea cried. "I want to go home."

"Marcel, take her to the sauna, will you? I think the air will do her good."

"Pleasepleasepleasenonono." Bea's objections only amplified as Marcel scooped her up over his shoulder. Her hands slammed against his back, bare feet kicked at his chest, yet none of it seemed to make a difference.

"Don't worry, Bea. We're here to help you." Linda waved to her client with a smile. The tips of her teeth jutted from her mouth and dug into her own gums. "You'll leave this place feeling like a brand new you."

Bea screamed as she drove the spike into Marcel's back. His grip slackened. The woman wormed away and thumped to the ground. She didn't dare look back at either of the employees. She ran. The wooden floor slapped under her bare feet. Finally, she reached the frosted door and threw it open. A pool took up most of the room. On both sides of this were hot tubs, and a sauna was by the innermost wall. Windows overlooked the surrounding forest and promised escape. She darted forward, but a tug on her hair sent a burning sensation up her scalp and stopped her. Another pull and a fist was up to her face, holding a wad of hair as it dragged her forward.

Marcel pulled her across the floor while Bea clawed at his wrist. He reached the metal door of the sauna. A digital thermometer with red lettering on the door read 175°F. He opened it and flung Bea inside.

The air was oppressive. It seemed to stick to her skin, warded off only by the sheen of sweat that quickly accumulated. The room was square with wooden benches surrounding a recessed floor, inside of which were rocks. The whole room had a red glow, attributable to infrared lights on the ceiling. Bea heard beeping, which was continuous until it wasn't. The air became hot, then hotter, then unbearable. Just as Bea felt the urge to tear her skin to cool off, blisters began to form and the wound on her hand began to crackle. She scratched at a bubble until it popped. Underneath all of the clear liquid was smooth skin.

***

Linda held open the frosted door. "Thanks again for coming! We hope to see you again soon."

Bea waved to her massage therapist. "You *definitely* will. Take care, Lin."

The masseuse smiled, showing off rows of pristine white teeth.

"You as well, hun!"

The doorman beamed at the woman as she approached. "Have a good day, Ms! I hope to see you soon!"

Bea gave a grateful nod. "Take care." She pulled her phone from her pocket as she walked to the car. The lock screen was flooded with notifications from Diane. Missed calls and text messages alike glared up at her from the screen. Bea smiled as she typed out her response.

Thanks again, Dee! That was just what I needed. Next time, let's make it a girl's trip. My treat!

The Wedge

"This is it. This summer, I'm *really* gonna do it."

Megan nodded as her thumb slid down her *iPhone*'s screen. "Good luck with that."

The boy ignored his sister's bemused tone. If he were to retort, she'd probably snap back with something smart, something already hammering against his skull: *Why don't you stop saying that, get your ass out of the sand, and do it already?*

The Wedge separated floaty-users from the big kids. The challenge was too daunting for most children and most teens were too cool to relive it. On the far side of the lake, just by the net that sectioned off the swimming area, was a floating dock with a diving board. Teens loved to lounge on it and watch the younger kids splash about with their trademarked sneers. He wasn't a strong enough swimmer to make it out there. Besides, he'd be shunned off the dock.

The giant inflatable in the middle of Turtleback Lake's swim zone was the perfect compromise. It had neon yellow sides with green tops. The float was equipped with a balance beam, a trampoline, and a rock wall mountain. The Wedge was a lip off the peak. Little kids would huddle on the trampoline as they watched their older, braver siblings cannonball from the summit. He used to watch Megan scale the rock wall, clinging to the rubber pegs as her friends pulled her to the top. After she jumped, she'd radiated a greatness he longed to replicate.

"This is it," he reminded himself. He pushed off of the sand, brushing the grains off his legs and blue and neon green swim trunks. "You better watch."

Megan shrugged, not looking up from her phone. "Whatever, just be careful, Conner. That thing's slippery."

Squeals from the water's edge caught his attention. His baby sister, Molly, was tottering from the base of a mini-slide to a large plastic turtle. Vanessa picked the child up and placed her on its shell. Molly treated it like a drum. When she saw her brother march toward the water, she pointed and bounced in her seat. "Nonner!"

"Hi, Moley-Poley." Conner approached the turtle. Deceptively warm water lapped at his ankles. "Vanessa, is it cool if I go on the

Wedge?"

Vanessa crossed her arms over her chest. "You've been on that thing before, right?"

"Uh-huh," he lied. "I'm just gonna hop off and come back."

"Whatever. Have you seen your father?"

"Nuh-uh. I think he's back at the campsite with Uncle Pete." He ignored the woman's muttering about being stuck with three kids as he waded into the water. He'd never understood the philosophy of diving right in. The shock of the water, especially lake water, seemed to linger under the skin until you truly adjusted. Conner was up to his waist relatively fast. The sand before that had lots of algae and rocks that made it uncomfortable to stand on. Only once he was ready would he inch forward, wait, and repeat. He looked downward to make sure he didn't step on anything, but as the water became deeper, he couldn't see more than a few inches down.

Splash.

Little girls playing mermaid ruined his preparation with a man-made tidal wave. "Hey, watch it!"

A little girl raised her hand in apology before another kid tackled her.

The Wedge loomed. Conner had once heard Dad speculate to Uncle Pete that it couldn't be any higher than six feet. The actual drop, according to Megan, was much deeper, because the camp people had to dig in the muck for a safer diving spot. All of this sloshed through his mind as he doggy-paddled to the inflatable. He couldn't, no, *wouldn't* bring himself to look at his destination. *Just take it one part at a time. You've got this.* There was a step just below the trampoline's side that helped kids get up onto the float. He grimaced as his foot made contact with the slimy surface and hopped up onto the trampoline to avoid it. A little boy bounced with his brother at the opposite side, but the vibrations made no impact on Conner.

The bounce and rock wall were separated by an inflatable gap that sunk into the water when stood on. A rope hung down the mountain's face. Conner grabbed it and hoisted his foot up to a plastic rock. It slipped back down. He instead focused on grabbing handholds, assuring himself the footholds would follow. The space for his fingers to grip onto was thin. He had to claw his way up by digging his nails into tiny grooves and standing on tippy toes on footholds.

At the summit was Mattie. That wasn't his real name, but Conner had long forgotten that. He was sitting in the middle of the peak with his one-man audience, Dean. His father, Mr. Matlock, owned the place, and Mattie didn't have enough imagination to act any other way. Picture a snotty, spoiled kid who looked down on those that dared to give his father income and you have Mattie Matlock. Dean had even less of an identity than his friend, if possible. He would just nod at everything the other said in between kisses to the ground Mattie walked on.

It would be best to ignore them, but the only other thing to concentrate on was the fall. Mattie's shark eyes (the kind that seemed all black, no pupil, except his were a deep brown) locked onto potential prey. Conner knew he would only have one chance to deflect the incoming barrage of wickedness. "Dontcha got something better to look at?"

Mattie's head cocked to the side. "I'm just waiting."

"For what?"

"For you to chicken out, that's what."

Conner puffed out his chest. Mattie was bigger and possibly older, but he wouldn't let that intimidate him. "I'm not gonna chicken out. I'm gonna do it, just you watch."

"Well? I'm waiting."

"Yeah," Dean chimed in. "I'm waitin' too."

His legs didn't seem to understand the assignment. His knees stayed rooted to the plastic, unshifting. *C'mon, don't be a baby, don't be a baby.* Conner shuffled on his knees to the ledge. Even with the motion of the water below, the sunshine made the water seem like concrete. A girl near the Wedge's base pointed upward and warned of an incoming jump. The surrounding kids cleared the area and waited for the splash to signal a return to their antics. His knees wouldn't move anymore. Even the breeze at his back seemed to urge him forward, but he refused.

Mattie snorted. "Told ya he wouldn't do it."

Conner shuffled on his knees with baby steps to spin around and face his accuser. "I don't see *you* rushin' to jump!"

"Just face it. You're a..." He paused, rolling insults around in his mouth like a jawbreaker. "A Chicken Little!"

Dean chortled.

"At least I don't have a *girly* name."

To boys on the cusp of teenhood, this accusation was particularly damning. "You take that back!"

Conner's ten-year-old pride was bruised enough. He wouldn't back down off the ledge, and he wouldn't back down from a verbal lashing. "Ma*ddy*."

Mattie retorted with the most malicious thing he could think of: he bounced. Dean followed suit. Conner tried to dig his fingers into the inflatable, but there was too much air in it. As he reached for the rope, Mattie punctuated his performance with a push.

The feeling of air flooding to his stomach was instantaneous. The icy water seized him. As he sunk lower, he could feel the temperature fall with him, the cold becoming more intrusive. His nose stung. His lungs burned. Conner opened his eyes.

Another boy looked back through empty sockets. One of his eyes was missing, while another dangled at his cheek. A minnow nipped at the dangling, consequence-free bait. The rest of the boy's body was surrounded in a murky haze, until a hand reached out from within it. Conner screamed. Water rushed down his throat and reduced his cry to bubbles. He thrashed absently in the water for something to grip onto. His legs kicked and kicked, yet the surface seemed no closer.

The dead boy lifted a skeletal finger to his lips.

A hand grabbed his arm and hoisted him up to the surface. He sputtered against his savior's chest and spat out lake water as he coughed. He looked up to see Megan smoothing his hair back. She glowered up at the Wedge. "Wait until I tell your parents, you little shit!"

Mattie and Dean snickered amongst themselves but made no reply.

Megan made her way back to shore. When the water was deep, she held her brother's head at her shoulder. As soon as she could walk, she carried him.

A lifeguard stood ankle deep, red life-raft hanging limply at his side. "Do you need any —"

"Move it," Megan snarled. He complied. She brought Conner back to their spot, placing her brother in her beach chair and kneeling beside him in the sand. It was only then he realized his sister was still in her sundress. Her phone lay face down in the sand. Black streaks of eyeliner gave her vertical whiskers. "Thank God, thank God you're okay. What happened?"

"Mattie pushed —"

"I saw *that*. I was getting ready to whack the little twerp, but then you didn't pop up."

Conner scanned the crowd, then the Wedge. He couldn't see his assailant anymore. *Who's the chicken now, jerk?*

"Noooooonnnnnerrr!" Molly tottered over as fast as she could. Vanessa sauntered behind her. The toddler clambered onto her brother's chest and hid her face in it. When she lifted her head, he saw a dribble of tears and snot mixed in with the residual water. "Nonner okay?"

"I'm okay, Molly."

With the baby satiated, Megan whirled on Vanessa. "Where the fuck were *you* when he was drowing?"

"I got the lifeguard," she replied, gesturing to the teen boy resuming his post. "What more did you want?"

"Some help dragging him out would've been *great*."

Vanessa slipped right into what his sister once dubbed a *Queen Beech face*. "You're not allowed to speak to me this way, Megan."

"Oh, I'm *sorry* I'm upset. My baby brother was *drowning!*"

"And what was I supposed to do with your baby *sister*, Megan? Leave her in the sand and hope she didn't drown too?" The elder woman shook her head. "Wait until your father hears about this. *You should have been out there with him.*"

Conner could see every word his sister wanted to scream swell beneath her lips. Instead of saying any of them, Megan reached a hand down to her brother. "C'mon, Con. I think you should lay down for a while."

The boy eased Molly off of his lap before standing. He refused the towel his elder sister tried to drape over his shoulders. Instead, he kicked on his *Croc* flip-flops and made his way back to the cabin.

As soon as the beach ended, grass took its place. There were some picnic tables to navigate before he could get to the dirt packed road. The whole campsite was one big loop. If you stuck to the road, you could pass all the campsites and find all the amenities you needed.

Conner heard Megan's sandals slapping against the road before he saw her. She placed a hand on his shoulder. "Seriously, are you okay?"

"Guess so. Mattie's a real prick though."

Megan laughed. "Where'd you hear that?"

"Dad."

"Figures."

The *crinkle-slap* of shoes against the road filled the silence. Sunlight filtered down through the trees, making the leaves seem like they were glowing. He could already feel the sun baking the water off his skin.

"I think I saw something in the water. Another boy." The idea seemed childish on land, like a kid's excuse for not going into the deep end. Yet every time he blinked; he could feel those empty sockets boring into him.

"No one was nearby when you went under," Megan countered.

"It wasn't a regular boy. He was *dead,* like a zombie or somethin', but he didn't seem mean. He just shushed me, like this." He brought his index finger to his lips.

Megan bit her bottom lip. "I think you need some rest, Con."

"What? You don't believe me?"

"I do." She sighed. "But you also went through something scary. Lots of times that makes your imagination show you scary things."

Conner couldn't find it in him to argue. The adrenaline of life re-gifted had lost its sway, and all he could feel were his burning, winded lungs. *A nap will set me straight.* When they made it back to the camper, he ignored his dad's greeting and the beginning of Megan's *Vanessa is such a bitch* rant.

The doorway opened up to a small kitchen with a dinette across from it. The latter could be converted into a bed for an extra guest. The closed-off master bedroom was to his right. At the left end of the camper were the bathroom and bunk beds. He crawled into the bottom bunk without bothering to change out of his bathing suit. Sleep enveloped him as fast as the water had.

Conner was beneath the lake's surface. He knew this because of how the fractured rays of light drifted downwards visibly in the space around him. There were no sounds of splashing from above, no fish swimming by. Only the boy. He was the only thing that could be seen with any clarity. The whole corpse was visible now. A metal wire passed through the hole between the leg bones. Farther down, he could just make out the top of the stake that anchored the float to the ground below it.

"Are you stuck?" Water did not intrude into his lungs as he spoke.

The other boy's chin bobbed up and down.

"Do you need help?"

The boy repeated the motion.

"I can try." Conner attempted to move forward, but an invisible barrier kept him away. He tried to stretch his arm past it, through it, but nothing worked.

The corpse shook his head as the sound of laughter sent ripples through the water.

Laughter buzzed around him. The camper was dark, but as soon as he stood up, he could see the fire outside. Conner threw a hoodie over his head and pulled on some pajama pants. When he got to the door, he slipped on his flip-flops and snatched the flashlight from the counter.

Dad was slapping his knee at some raunchy joke told by Uncle Pete. Megan shook her head as she scrolled through her phone. It was only when she noticed her brother that her attention shifted and she nudged her father, who smiled. "Hey, bud. Heard you had a nasty slip."

"He was *pushed,* Dad," Megan corrected.

The man waved her off. "Van said she spoke to the lifeguard after you two came back. He said Mattie must've just been playing rough, and you slipped. No shame in that, Con."

"Guess so." Conner shrugged. "Is it okay if I go and catch some frogs?"

"*Ick.*" Vanessa was at the picnic table with her daughter. "Those things are disgusting. You shouldn't be touching them."

"Aw, lay off, hun." Dad gave her the same wave he gave to Megan. "The kid's had a rough day. Go have fun, just check in every once in a while."

"Don't you *dare* bring those frogs back here, Conner," Vanessa warned. Dad did not jump to his defense this time. He was engrossed with his brother's joke once more. "You'll be in that camper for the rest of this trip if you do."

"I won't." Conner tussled Molly's hair before he walked down the path. He started out slow. He shined his flashlight through the brush on either side of him. Frogs scattered when the light brushed over them. Any other night, he'd chase them, oblivious to the dangers of ticks and poison ivy, but tonight, he had a mission. Every now and again he would cast a look back down the path to ensure none of the adults followed him. He expected Megan to interrupt his false search any minute now, demanding that he get his rest. She never came. So, he ran.

At night the moon existed in two places simultaneously: Turtleback Lake and the sky. The moon's radiance was the former's only disturbance. Even the cool breeze seemed to avoid the water, as no ripples marred the surface. The chill was his only deterrent. No lifeguards were on duty at night. The sign declaring *No Swimming After Dark* by the snack stand remained his only other obstacle. Conner pulled off his hoodie, then his pants, and abandoned the flashlight with them in the sand. Before he waded in, he grabbed a rock that was slightly bigger than his fist. He marched into the water up to his chest and began doggy-paddling. Night was a dangerous time to dawdle here. He knew snakes came out at night, and he suspected a big shark was waiting below the dark waters.

He only had a general idea where the anchor was. He paddled around the area he fell into earlier, groping with his free hand for a line. Swimming with the rock proved laborious, so he would often take breaks and stop swimming, treading water long enough to catch his breath. It was on one of these breaks that he kicked something hard. He lowered his foot. Once he found it again, he ran his foot up and down the cord to test its length. "That's gotta be it. Alright… Okay." He took a deep breath and dove under the water. He grabbed the line with his free hand and used it to guide him into the darkness. Visibility did not let up. He clutched at his rock, hoping it would be adequate protection from the monsters likely lurking below him. Anxiety gnawed at the back of his mind and the cold latched onto his bones. Just as his lungs began to burn, he felt something extend around the line. One side was thick, the other was thin. The metal cord ran through the narrow gap between them. The thinner side felt sharp, like it was cracked.

Oxygen demanded Conner resurface. He clutched onto his rock as he kicked his way to the surface. "You can do this, you can do this." With another gulp, he descended. He swam faster with a general idea of how far down he needed to go. The metal cord brushed against his side on the way down. When he reached the obstruction again, he swung his arm back and knocked the rock into the bone. Again he tried, but with similar results: nothing happened.

He breached. "The water's slowin' me down, but don't worry! I'll getcha, okay?" Another breath, another dive. This time, he banged the rock into the bone in shorter, harder bursts. *Crack.* Conner dropped his rock and restrained the need to yelp. Instead, he reached out to touch the bone, only to find open water. He struggled to the surface for the last time. The wind stopped. He could feel nothing but the dense summer air press against his cheeks… and a hand grab his wrist. He gasped. The hand made no effort to pull. In a flicker of moonlight, he could see the empty eyes of the corpse staring up at him. His lower jaw, which was mostly skeletal, opened. "D–do… Do you wanna go to the beach?"

The corpse's mouth opened and closed.

"I'll take that as a yes." Conner scooped downward to get his arm under the other boy's armpit before kicking for the shore. As soon as he could walk, he planted his feet in the sand. The corpse followed suit. They walked until the water lapped at their ankles. Conner noticed the other wouldn't move any further.

The dead boy stood tall, even though one of his legs was cracked. A few strands of human hair were mixed with algae strands. Whatever skin he had left was gray and puffy. He pushed his eye back into its socket with a skeletal hand. "...Thank...you..." His words were a gargle. Bubbles seemed to pop in his throat with each syllable he pronounced.

Conner's mouth opened once, twice, but sound refused to follow.

"...Been there...so long..." His chin shifted toward the water. "...They put the...peg in the soil...through my leg...dug me up..."

"H-how — How did you die?"

The corpse's head whipped toward him. His eye popped right back out of his skull. "...Never...ask me...that..."

"Sorry." Conner shivered. "Do you have a name?"

"...Once...I did...But I don't...know anymore..."

"Can I call you something?"

"...If...you need to..."

The living boy tilted his head from one side to the other. "How about Guppy?"

"...That is...a fish..."

"Yup. But Dad always tells me that if I spend too much time in the water, I'll turn into a fish. And, well, you've been in there a while, right?" Conner kicked at the water, waiting for a response, but he got none. "Do you want me to bury you or something? Maybe go get the police? Or my Dad?"

Guppy shook his head. A strand of algae splashed into the water below. "...My place...is here..."

"Oh, okay." Conner looked about the lake until his eyes landed on the solitary mountain. "Listen, now that you're free 'n all, do you think... Would you help me with something?"

The corpse nodded.

"Well, see, there's this kid —"

"...The one...who pushed you...?"

It was Conner's turn to nod.

"...I think...I know...where you are...going with this..."

***

Dad was too busy with Uncle Pete and Vanessa was too busy with Molly to notice Conner walk back into the water. Megan began to voice an objection, which he silenced with a thumbs up. He could feel her eyes on him as he swam out to the Wedge and made his ascent.

"Chicken Little's back, Dean." Mattie nudged his companion. "Ready for another swim?"

"Sure." Conner shrugged and stood to his feet. "But, see, I was thinkin' yesterday, and I don't think I've ever seen you jump off this thing."

Mattie snorted. "How else do you think I get down from here, dummy?"

"The rock wall." Conner motioned behind him with his head. "When d'ya think you're gonna head down?"

Dean was looking at Mattie expectantly now. The latter boy bristled. "When I don't have to throw you down there."

"So, if I jump, you will too?"

"Yeah."

"Okay, sure." Conner wobbled over to the edge. "See ya at the bottom." When he jumped, he was sure he heard Megan screech. The sound was quickly replaced with water rushing past his ears. This time, he had plugged his nose for the fall. Cold brushed his cheeks like a doting mother. Opening his eyes showed the shadows of kicking feet and the mossy underbelly of the inflatable. He resurfaced with ease. "Whenever you're ready, *Chicken Little*."

Mattie hesitated. Conner couldn't tell whether it was Dean or pride that sent him over the side, but he came down screaming. He also came up screaming. Conner could make out Guppy below the surface, his hands clutched to the Mattie's arms, his mouth opening and closing. Mattie shook himself free yet made no effort to escape. He locked eyes with his former victim, silently pleading for help.

"That's my friend, Guppy. We were talking last night about how tired everyone is of you being a jerk."

Bubbles popped above Guppy's head. He then surfaced, lunging for Mattie. Conner watched his adversary scramble away, splashing as he pushed himself through the water. Guppy did not follow. He gave his accomplice a nod before sinking back to the depths. Conner locked eyes with his sister standing at the lapping shore. Megan gave a thumbs up. He cupped his hands over his mouth and yelled, "I *told* you! This summer, I *finally* did it!"

Shock

This story was originally published in Dark Matter Magazine, Halloween Special Issue 002, October 2022

The man only known as Red was greeted with a human doll and muffled screams from upstairs.

Red had met his host, Richard (username *rhannedy75*), on *Craigslist.* The outdated site was about as close to the black market as the average person could venture. With shoppers diverted to Amazon and (less commonly) eBay, those with questionable wares ranging from hookers to organs to willing victims of crime took over, waiting for buyers to stumble upon their advertised services.

Red (username *j4n6QhR4Txy2*), offered "medical services, pending payment." He didn't ask when Richard offered him money, he didn't ask when he had to drive out into The-Land-With-No-Reception, and he didn't ask about the smell of roadkill when the bespectacled man opened the door. But when he saw what awaited him, he couldn't hold his tongue.

"What the *fuck* is that?"

"*Shh!* She can hear you." Richard pushed up his horn-rimmed glasses and walked toward the couch, standing behind the doll. "This is my wife, Rebecca."

Red had seen people shot, people iced in a tub with their kidneys out, but never anything like what Richard called "Rebecca." The smell of moldy cold cuts was proof of her authenticity, but nothing screamed human about her. Her eyes were glass. Eye shadow and eyeliner were smudged and poorly applied. Her skin looked plastic, not in the way corpses in funeral homes do, but in a way that made her face look covered in plaster, eyes bulging out like a goldfish. Her body was wrapped in rags, and a blanket was thrown over her lap.

"What did you *do* to her?"

"Nothing." Richard leaned down to kiss Rebecca's head. The scalp of hair moved, clearly unattached. It might have looked more realistic if he'd put a mop or corn husks on her head. "You should have seen her before."

Red shook his head. "Look, man, her organs aren't going to be any good."

Richard cocked his head to the side, confused. His blue eyes reminded Red of the frozen corpses found up on Mount Everest: cold, gone from this world. "You aren't here for Rebecca," he replied.

The noise from upstairs continued.

"I dunno, man. This don't feel right."

"Are you quitting?" Richard frowned. "You said you were accustomed to these kinds of operations."

"Yeah, but this shit's *fucked.*"

Richard didn't say anything. He clucked his tongue once, twice, three times. "I'll pay you double."

"You're bluffing."

Richard closed the distance between them. Red shifted his weight back, moving a leg with it, but an attack never came. Instead, his employer fell to his knees, hands grasping at his ankles, tugging at the hem. "Please, I'm begging you. You'll get all the money you want, all of it and more, just please, *please,* you have to trust me."

Usually when Red saw people beg, it was because he was holding a gun to their head, or a knife to their neck. But now, without the aid of either, he watched Richard's shoulders rise and fall, listened to his breath catch in his throat. Richard's tears fell on Red's sneakers, and Red ripped his foot away. He thought about kicking the man, but stopped himself before he ruined the deal.

Easy money. Just do what the sick fuck wants and take the cash.

"What do you want from her?" Red motioned with his head to the staircase and to the sound upstairs. The sound became a thump, followed by a low wail.

"Her brain. Everything else is yours."

"Man, murder wasn't a part of this deal!"

"No, you don't understand!" Richard scrambled to his feet. He wiped the tears from his eyes and gripped Red's shoulders. "I'm not *killing* her. She'll live again, she'll live through Rebecca. See, Rebecca had brain cancer. She doesn't have a brain now, but if she had one… I've read that electricity can recharge muscles, make them move again. If you read *Frankenstein* or… or… You'll see! She won't die, you'll see."

"You aren't paying me enough for this shit."

"You know how much these organs sell for separately, right? Imagine how much you can make from *all of them.*" Richard gripped

Red's shoulders tighter. "How much would an organ like the heart go for, huh? Or *both* kidneys?"

Red shoved him away, but he had to admit, the man's pitch got him thinking. A kidney went for about $25,000. But a heart? He'd seen those go for a hundred grand. It wouldn't take much to kill the woman upstairs, and the payout would be huge.

Let the weirdo have his brain, Red thought. *I'm gonna get paid.*

"You got ice?"

"I went and bought a few bags this morning. I thought you might…"

"Good. Go set up the bathtub. I'll take care of the rest."

Along the staircase wall were pictures of Richard and his wife. Rebecca, in life, had olive skin and blonde hair that fell in rivers over her shoulders. Sometimes she wore it in French braids. As Red ascended, the pictures of Rebecca changed. First, her hair was cut shorter, then later, her head was wrapped in a scarf.

Every door upstairs was closed, but the sounds of terror were hard to misplace. He walked past two doors on his right in favor of the last door on his left. Red twisted the knob and entered.

Oh fuck.

His intended victim was tied to the bedpost by her wrists. Her body hung off one side, and her bare feet were kicking desperately against the carpet. Her heels were bleeding from the constant friction, and it appeared as though her right shoulder was badly dislocated, the bone protruding at an odd angle. A filthy rag was stuffed inside her mouth.

As Red approached, her kicks became more furious. She was exhausted and terrified, a dangerous combination, kicks thrown at random with no goal in mind other than survival. She pulled on her restraints, which exacerbated her injury and made her muffled shrieks louder.

Red approached with his hands outstretched. Her feet met his hands once, twice, as he did his best to catch them, like a bear fishing for river salmon. As soon as Red caught one of her feet, he yanked. He wanted to get the woman to the ground and eliminate her leverage, but she rolled to her side in an evasive maneuver right as Red moved to climb on top of her.

The easiest way is to break her neck. Just one quick twist and she's gone.

Red gripped her cheeks. Her legs flailed behind him, and tears and snot ran down her cheeks. She begged with her eyes for mercy even as they began to bulge from their sockets. Red gripped harder and then quickly twisted her neck violently in an attempt to snap it. He twisted with no luck. And then he twisted again.

Why won't she die?

His victim, still very much alive, tried once more to escape, but she didn't have the strength to succeed.

Red grabbed her head again and —

"Don't!" It was Richard. He was standing in the doorway, where he had dropped the bag of ice onto the floor.

At the sight of him, the tied-up woman peed herself.

"You might damage the brain stem."

"Then why don't you do it yourself?" Red snapped.

Richard clucked his tongue. "Why don't you go fill up the bathtub? It's right across the hall."

"Whatever you say," Red replied. He grabbed the bag of ice from the floor on his way out.

As he left the room, he heard Richard humming a familiar tune, though the name of the song escaped him. He threw open the bathroom door, drew back the shower curtain, tossed the cheap shampoo on the ground, and poured the ice into the tub. The sound of crushed ice being dumped muted the sounds of the woman's screams in the other room, which rose in crescendo and then fell silent.

"...lucky I'm in love with my best friend, dah-da da dah-dah de da da..."

Richard entered the bathroom with the woman slumped over his shoulder. His blue button-up was stained crimson.

Red couldn't quite tell what Richard had done to finish her off. There was blood — so much blood — but no visible wounds.

Her chest rose and fell.

"She's still breathing," Red said with surprise.

"It'll give you a bit longer with the organs, won't it?"

Red sighed. "Go get the coolers from my truck."

Richard nodded, turning on his heel. "...lucky I'm in love in every way, lucky to have stayed where we have stayed..."

***

Red took the brain out last.

Richard looked on in chastised silence (he'd been told to shut up on more than one occasion), standing with hands in his pockets, back pressed against the wall, eyes fixed in glassy reverie. Occasionally, he would hum, but he would quickly stop at the first sign of Red tensing up.

Each organ went one after the other into the coolers. Blood dripped down the sides.

Red came to the brain and paused before proceeding. He looked over his shoulder at Richard. "When is this...this surgery of yours happening?"

"As soon as humanly possible."

Red set his jaw and slid his tongue over his teeth. He had sewn the woman back up where he could. The chest was impossible to fix, considering he had to go in with garden shears to crack her ribs, and with the skull...well, he just placed the top back on like the lid to a jar. He put the brain in a bowl of ice and handed it to his benefactor.

Richard held the bowl and regarded the brain with reverence.

"I...I can't thank you enough for this."

"Don't mention it."

"I mean it, I–"

"I mean it, too. Don't mention it. *Ever.*"

"Oh. Gotcha." Richard smiled sheepishly. "Want to make an extra thousand?"

"I'm not getting rid of the body for you." The tub was quite literally a bloodbath, and it would take more than bleach to sanitize the room. "Do that shit yourself."

"No, no, I just...Well, I could use some help with Rebecca's procedure." Richard pinched the frame of his glasses with his thumb and middle finger and adjusted them on his face. "I understand if I've used too much of your time already. I'm sure you're a busy man."

No way I'm sticking around for this shitshow.

"I'll pass."

"Please? I just, well, I'm not sure I can lift the battery. I'm pretty sure it weighs as much as I do."

"And what are you going to do with this battery, huh? Attach it to her and watch her fry?"

"Something like that. But she won't fry. You'll see. I've prepped her body. She looks better than before."

Red pressed his lips together. "An extra thousand?"

"Yes, yes." Richard was already out the bathroom door, trotting down the stairs.

Red followed.

"The battery's in the shed. Just go out the front, you'll see it in the yard," Richard took the blanket from Rebecca's lap and threw it over the back of the couch. He took her in his arms and eased her onto her back. He kneeled next to the couch, holding her hand in his, whispering God-knows-what to her.

Fucking creep.

Once alone outside, Red debated leaving, but decided against it. Today was like a car accident and he couldn't bring himself to look away. He lugged the battery and some jumper cables in from the shed, as instructed.

Back inside, Rebecca's wig of hair lay on the ground. Her skull was empty.

"Where'd her brain go?" Red asked. He set the battery down.

"They took it out when she was embalmed," Richard replied. He let go of Rebecca's hand. "You know, the Egyptians used to pull the brain out from the nose."

"Gross." Red plugged the battery into the nearest outlet. "Look, man, this ain't gonna work."

"It worked in *Frankenstein*." Richard connected a jumper cable to the battery, kissed his wife's brow, hesitated, then clamped the cable to her arm. At first, there was a sudden jolt. Then smoke. Then flames. The fabric wrapping her arms, legs, everywhere, was instantly alight. Rebecca's cheap makeup melted from her face.

Richard didn't scream, but Red noticed every ounce of terror prepared to leap from his throat. Red yanked the plug from the outlet, but the damage was already done. The fire spread to the couch, then to the blanket draped across the back. Richard dashed from the room. As Red stomped out the gathering flames, Richard returned with a fire extinguisher. The fire was stopped with a cloud of CO_2.

Rebecca's corpse was destroyed. One glass eye had burst, and with the rags burned away, Red could now see bone. A strange liquid seeped into the couch.

"What have I done?" Richard whispered. He reached an arm out toward Rebecca but withdrew it immediately. "My God, what have I done?"

"Hate to say I told you so." Red crossed his arms over his chest.

Richard didn't move, didn't turn to sneer at him. His shoulders slumped. "I…I killed that girl upstairs, didn't I? She's really gone."

"Yeah."

Red leaned down and clapped Richard on the shoulder. "I'm out of here, man. Good luck with all this."

"I can bring Julia back," Richard mumbled.

"What?"

"Julia, the girl from upstairs, I can bring her back. I just need to lower the wattage, maybe even get a better conductor…" Richard began to laugh, then stopped. He turned to Red.

"How would you like to make an extra ten grand?"

Snuff

All Rachels and Ralphs handled their prescribed deaths differently. Some cried, others were chipper, but most fixated on the miasma of their thoughts, focused on a point absent from reality. This Rachel fell into the latter category. Alan had even worried she'd taken some pills to mellow herself out; a big no-no for these cases. The whole procedure could be called off. He assuaged his worry by waving a hand in front of her face, peeling the glaze of thought from her eyes.

"Do you mind?" Her tone balanced on a line between defeat and exhaustion.

"Just making sure you're with us." Alan gestured to the men behind him. Louie was adjusting the lights, making sure their subject was properly illuminated, while Tom was putting together his boom mic. "We're just about done."

"Yeah, okay." The woman sat up straighter on her bed. The Rachel/Ralphs' home, the doctors attested, was the most comfortable place for their film. This, of course, came with its detractions. Dressers, desks, bookshelves, and nightstands all served as barriers for equipment and proper framing. Louie was in constant obscenity-fueled battles with the dysfunctional lighting of the average home.

Alan grabbed the black swivel chair from her desk and pulled it next to the bed. A gray bathrobe with moons and stars fell off the chair's back in the process. The director was quick to replace it. "Alright, Rachel, I'm gonna explain how things're going down today. You listenin'?"

"My name isn't Rachel."

"I know, I know, don't bust my balls." Alan ran a hand over his shaved head, allowing stubborn remnants to scratch at his palm. "This makes things easier for everyone, yeah?"

Rachel squinted at Alan before flopping back on her mountain of pillows. "Whatever gets us through this, I guess."

"Great." He clapped his hands together and leaned forward in the chair. "So, what happens is we leave you in here for five minutes with the camera on. Make sure to speak loud, 'cause Tommy won't have his mic over you, okay? Anyways, this is your chance to say your piece without us here. You can say your goodbyes, cry, verbally fuck everyone, what do I care? It's your five minutes. By then, the Doc should be here. That's when we get rollin', you die, and we all get outta here in time for dinner. Sound good?"

"As good as it's going to get."

"Great." Alan pushed off of the chair's arms. "We'll be in the hall. And remember, five minutes, capiche?"

"Got it." Rachel rested her left ear against her shoulder, looking past the director at the camera. Chestnut hair tumbled down her shoulder as her head shifted direction.

Alan snapped at his crew and they all shuffled out the door. The hall was relatively dark, with the only light coming from under Rachel's doorway and a lamp down the hall. Even so, he could just make out his v-neck hairline and how far his cheeks dared to protrude past his goatee in the hall mirror. He turned to his crew, his whisper coming out like a growl. "Do either of youse two know why the Doc ain't here yet?"

Louie frowned at his phone. Alan always thought he looked like a fish when he did that. His wide upper lip stretched down too far, giving him an elongated triangle over a short chin. "He hasn't texted me back yet. Want me to give him a call?"

"We got a girl ready to die in there, Lou. What do you *think* you should do?" He ran a hand over his head once more. "Tell the Doc to hurry his ass up while you're at it. The poor kid's been waitin' long enough."

"I'm going outside, too. I could use a smoke." Tom, even when talking at full volume, never projected. It took Alan two years not to *uh-huh* everything the sound mixer said.

"Make it snappy. You got *four* minutes."

Louie gave a mock salute before he led his friend down the hall.

***

Each patient was required to watch the prior year's recorded assisted suicides before doctors would consider offering it. It was meant to be a deterrent to the new law, but they applied regardless. Getting approved required navigating bureaucratic mazes straight from Kafka. Many doctors were reluctant, especially in cases with younger patients like Rachel.

Alan first saw her at the doctor's hearing. Five white-coats sat at a long wooden table with Rachel on the other side. Her hands were clasped before her, and her hair was tied back into a loose bun. By his judgment, she couldn't be any older than thirty-five, yet here she was, pleading her case for death.

He was one of three directors employed by the hospital. They were seated along the back wall in leather chairs, functioning as isolated observers as the doctors discussed their next production. Alan didn't know either of his cohorts very well. One was a younger guy who always found the most inappropriate time to sniffle. The other, for all he knew, was already dead, and wheeled from grave to meeting room for each client.

"Ms. Kent," one of the doctors began. Alan could never tell which one spoke at these proceedings. They didn't talk to the directors, not even on set, but when they did talk, each doctor had a curated tone of professional apathy. "We *very* rarely approve cases for patients as young as yourself. And with the probability that you'll be able to live a few more years with intervention—"

"I'm sorry, Doctor, but I don't call that living." Rachel's voice pinched off her tears. "I don't want to live just to see myself deteriorate."

"Even so, Ms. Kent, assisted euthanasia is *only* to be administered when nothing else can be done. Medications exist to ward off the side effects and there are clinical trials you can take part in."

"But do any of these things ever actually *help*?"

"They are measures to keep the patient comfortable, and in some instances, delay the progression."

"But they don't cure it, do they?"

"No, Ms. Kent. There is no cure for Alzheimer's."

Rachel shook her head. The trail of a single tear caused her right cheek to glisten in the hospital's fluorescent lighting. She wiped the remnant of weakness away with the back of her hand before clenching it again. "I've been doing research, you know, to try to find comfort in facts. I don't have anything left to cling onto anymore. Only five or six percent of people get it at my age. I shouldn't have this, I *should* have more time, but I don't. I'm not here trying to make a precedent; I'm here trying to preserve some fucking dignity." She stood from her chair. The doctors' heads moved with her. "I hope you'll find some mercy."

The younger director sniffled, and the doctors clustered their chairs together as Rachel left the room. Alan watched the woman as she walked out. She didn't cry again.

***

"What do you mean he can't get here? What the hell am I supposed to tell her?" Alan ran his hand down his head before he gestured at the door.

"Apparently his car broke down. His phone just got charged enough to reach out to us." Louie made his fish face. "I can go get him, obviously, but Rachel's going to have to wait *at least* a half an hour."

Alan groaned. "Look, do what you gotta do, alright?"

"I'll get back here as soon as I can."

"Yeah, yeah, yeah." Alan scrubbed his hands over his face and up his head. "Take Tom with ya. The last thing she needs is the big lug mutterin' at her."

Tom didn't acknowledge the abuse. He was already tottering down the hall after Louie.

Alan took one deep breath, then another, before returning to the woman's bedroom. "Listen, kid, we have a little delay. Doc's having car trouble."

Rachel's eyebrows furrowed. "It's still happening today, right?"

"We don't put stuff like this off. It wouldn't be right, y'know?"

Rachel sighed. "Thank God."

Alan pulled the swivel chair toward the foot of the bed. When the robe fell this time, he curled it up into a ball and put it on the desk. The chair squeaked when he leaned back.

Rachel made an effort to sit up straighter against her pillows. "How long have you been doing this?"

"About three years."

"Do you like it?"

"It's a hell of a thing to try and like." He smoothed his hand over his head. "But, sure, in some ways I do."

"I see." She tilted her head, inviting her hair to spill onto her chest. "It's just that you said giving everyone the same name made things easier."

Alan shrugged. "Death is never easy. No one likes watchin' it, 'cept for some sick fucks. So, yeah, I guess I try to look at it a different way. How else am I gonna get any sleep at night?" He picked at the arm of the chair. There was a worn patch near the front of it. "It's not like I'm doin' anythin' wrong. This is your ticket to Heaven or Nirvana or a hole in the ground. Whatever you believe, it's peace, a mercy."

"For the patients, sure. But you must get some serious PTSD from all of this."

Alan's leg began to jiggle up and down, his heel jumping yet never hitting the floor. "Yeah, well, someone's gotta do it. And, not for nothin', you've watched the videos too, so you know how it is."

Rachel gripped her hands over her stomach. "I guess. They all had their own reasons and… I don't know. It was sadder than anything. Maybe I just think it's something I wouldn't put myself through if I didn't have to."

Alan returned his hand to his head. "The way I look at it, this is far more rewardin' than the stuff I used to make. That was art, entertainment. Dontcha get me wrong, that has value too, but this is someone's memory we're talkin' about here. Shootin' it right, keepin' youse guys in good light, it's preservation. That's all there is to it."

Rachel's hair slid up and down her shoulder as she nodded. "Can I ask you a question?"

"Shoot."

"Do you think I'm doing the right thing?"

The combined weight of the question and her gaze stifled Alan. "That's not for me to answer. This is a really personal decision. But listen, if you are havin' doubts—"

"No." Rachel began stroking the back of her intertwined fingers with her thumb. Red bloomed through each digit. "No. There's no other way for me to go about this." Her gaze lost its intensity as it abandoned the ethereal. "Have you ever met anyone with Alzheimer's?"

Alan shook his head.

"My Nana had it. She fought *so* hard. Everything the doctors told her to do, anything they asked her to try, she agreed. She put *Post-It* notes all around the house. They were on light switches, above the couch, on the milk in the fridge. But you know what, it wasn't on? My PeePaw's picture. It was by her bed, and she'd kiss it every night before she went to sleep. And then one day… One day, she came into the living room holding it, and gave it to my dad. She said, 'Richard, why'd you put this in our room?' I think that's what broke him. She went into a home not long after."

Alan's mouth opened and closed. Words would only come out as breaths of air, as sorrowful looks.

"I couldn't do that, Alan. I couldn't live knowing that one day I could introduce myself to my own parents. I'm not that strong. I'm not... It's not..." Tears triumphed over speech. Rachel's breath refused to correct itself, serving only as a series of inhalations.

Alan stood from his chair and knelt at her side. "Sara, look at me a minute."

Rachel turned to look at him. She held a hand to her eyes to try to stop the tears. "You don't have to—"

"I know, but I want you to listen to me, got it?" Alan did not wait for assent. He placed a hand atop hers. "I just met you, but I want you to know that you're a fighter. You told me a sad story, but instead of ending on 'woe is me,' which would be normal, you're worried about your folks. You see what I'm sayin'? You're not weak just 'cause you can't handle something no one should have to go through. It's not easy to meet death in the ring. It takes a strong fighter. I need you to know that, Sara."

She smiled. A tear caught in the divot of her lips before dripping down her chin. "Thanks, Alan."

"You can call me Chuck."

Sara raised an eyebrow. "You use a fake name?"

"What can I say? It's an old show biz nickname. I won't bore you with the details. But you, Sara? You deserve to know who you're talking to."

Three taps sounded at the door. "We're ready when you are."

If you or a loved one are suffering from depression or suicidal thoughts, please know you are not alone.

US: Dial 1-800-273-8255 or text 741741
UK: 0800-689-5652
Alzheimer's Support Line
US: 1 (800) 272-3900
UK: 0333-150-3456

Rest in Peace

"What's the point of going if we can't take pictures?" E.J. Sharpe asked this not to his companion, but his neon-green adversary. The sign hung on a brick wall leading into the collection just after two signs regaling the Mütter Museum's history. It proclaimed:

Please refrain from any photography beyond this point. All of our specimens come from or represent the medicinal struggles of real people. We thank you for your compliance in respect of their memory.

"Seems like you'll just have to capture it all up here." Melody tapped her index finger against her temple twice.

Sharpe did not relent from his one-sided stare down. "It's just *unfair*. I—we—didn't come all this way to store it *up here*." Before he could repeat her gesture, the woman looped her arm around his and led him forward.

Two things were readily apparent as they passed into the museum: the wall of skulls and the annoyingly well-equipped security guard. The technology was a modern invader in the wood-clad room. The museum, according to the signs before his nemesis, was a former physician's college. The air of age and academia clung to the deep-brown walls. Without the macabre decor, the place had the potential to feel like a library; learning abundant in a cozy environment. At the center of the room was a cut out square. A brass rail ran along its rim. The stairs led downward to more exhibits. Aspiring doctors used to observe from above as their teachers did the actual work on cadavers. If this was the point of the bi-level room, then the aura of comfort tainted by gore and the smell of formaldehyde was as integral to the building as its foundation.

Overseeing it all was the guard, who looked away from his charge long enough to give the newcomers a courteous nod. The man had brown hair overridden with gray and an attentive gaze fixated on the monitor before him. The screen was segmented, showing multiple areas of the museum at once. Just when Sharpe thought there may be a blind spot, the feed switched to different locations. Melody's smile contrasted with his tight lipped acknowledgement. *If I'm lucky, there'll be a changing of the guard at some point.* Worse comes to worst, he could always circle back and time the feed's switches to coordinate a photography heist.

All plotting was erased when his wife stopped before the Soap Lady. Melody's lips were parted, and her head was hung in reverence as she inspected the exhibit. The corpse was an alarming juxtaposition to his initial suppositions, as he had assumed jarred organs and stripped skeletons would comprise most of the collection. Without proper signage, he could have mistaken her for an art piece; a clay sculpture molded in dark fantasy. The hair sold him on her validity. Blonde strands protruded from the body's casing, at times remaining imprisoned in decay and denied plumage. Strands that escaped this bondage draped against a glass slab. The substance caked over her body was almost black, with splotches of white along the torso, shoulders, and one arm. It rose in crags and leveled in valleys. The outer-layer was smooth nowhere except the head. The skull was covered with the taut mimicry of skin. The only deviation came at the crown of her scalp, where hair entangled in the muck. Only two instances here proved the substance's depth. The first were the eye sockets. The caverns accrued sediment, leveling off just before the rim, which gave the impression of flat brown eyes. The corpse's mouth was particularly jarring. Whether through *rigor mortis* or the process of her encapsulation, the Soap Lady's mouth was wide open. Her jaw was tilted to the right and fixed her mouth into an eternal scream. The realism of this effect was amplified by the coating in the throat. Only the bottom and back were covered, giving the illusion of a tongue and palette.

"It's incredible." Sharpe had an overwhelming urge to put his hand on the glass. "Melody, this is just the sort of thing I've been looking for."

She nodded. Her gaze was fixed on the informational plaques above the Soap Lady's enclosure. "Apparently they have no idea who she is or how she died. Isn't that crazy? You'd think with all the tech we have..." Melody dipped her chin to look at the corpse. "Poor thing."

"Yes, how tragic to be the star of a world-renowned museum." Sharpe ignored the slap to his arm as he took his *Moleskin* from his tan denim jacket. He picked a fuzz ball, likely from the fleece lining of his coat, from the pages and wrote *Soap Lady, scream, anonymous, lumpy* before returning it to his pocket. "It's really perfect."

Melody did not share in his enthusiasm. Her lips were pinched downward on the right side. "*She*, not *it*. You wouldn't want someone talking about you that way."

"I don't think she can hear me." He shrugged. "Besides, that's why you brought me here, isn't it? To observe all this stuff?"

"I'm sort of stuck with you," she chided as she moved towards Einstein's brain. "I didn't think you would objectify the dead. You should know better."

"What can I say? You knew my job when you said 'I do.'"

The conversation dwindled as they moved from the genius' brain to the wall of skulls. His notebook cycled in and out of his pocket as he took note of the specimens. Each had a year and method of death, a presumed age, and on most occasions, a name. He scribbled down the ones that intrigued him as his wife moved onto the wax models of skin diseases. There was no denying their grotesque nature, but Sharpe wasn't interested, not with *real* nightmares abound. Melody bent before the case, hands on her knees, studying the gangrene model. Her husband circled around and went down the stairs. He moved past the case housing a giant and a little person's skeleton in favor of the display behind them.

These bone figures had flat protrusions on and around their skeletons. Much like the Soap Lady, they were entrapped by their bodies. Certain areas were smooth as the plaster cast of the original Siamese twins located on the same floor. Other parts were jagged plates of armor covering and engulfing sections of bone. One had a head and neck permanently tilted to the left. The other had shoulders scrunched upwards, arms held plaintively before it. The plaque informed him that the pair had bone growth in their muscles, eventually restricting their movement and breath. *At least the Soap Lady could die first.*

A ringtone played somewhere in the museum. A group of teenagers passed, texting without looking up at the morbid realities around them. No security rushed these people, nor did the museum go into an automatic shutdown in the presence of a phone. *They can't really prove what you are doing, can they?* Sharpe pulled out his *Google Pixel* and opened his camera. He captured the skeletal pair. Nothing happened. "Well, isn't that something."

Sharpe was careful with his discovered leniency. He only took pictures of things that truly disturbed him: the Giant, the dermoid cyst, the corset women. This scrutiny became hard to maintain in the baby section. There was a skeleton that was crumpled together like a wad of paper. A plaster cast of a conjoined twin was the centerpiece. The babies shared a torso, with one set of head and arms being where the legs would normally be. The baby had three legs, with two on one hip, one on another. Just as he snapped a picture, he felt a tap on his shoulder. "Mel, can you believe the stuff that is — " Sharpe cut himself off when he took note of the overly-pungent customer service smile that greeted him. "Can I help you?"

"Hello, sir! I couldn't help but notice you were taking pictures." The woman only came up to his breast-bone, yet her authoritative power asserted her authority.

"Oh yeah. Sorry." Sharpe slipped his phone back into his coat pocket. "It won't happen again."

"Great!" The blonde tucked a strand from her bob behind her ear. "I'll just need to see you delete them."

He blinked. "I'll get around to it, okay? I'm trying to look at the exhibits."

"I understand that, sir, but if you don't do it now, you might forget to do it later." The woman still wore her forceful smile. "It should really only take a few seconds."

He clucked his tongue against the roof of his mouth. "Look, they're on my phone, right? Do you really have any say about what I do with stuff on it?"

Her look was patron-friendly venom. "No, sir, but I *do* have control over who stays in the museum. If you can't respect our rules, I'm afraid I will have to ask you to leave."

"Is there a problem here?" Melody weaved her way through the sporadic onlookers that were starting to amass and stood before her husband. Although he couldn't see her face, he could recognize the annoyance behind the veil of her stranger-approved perfectly-polite tone.

"I was just explaining to your friend that photography isn't allowed here, so if he doesn't delete his pictures, I'll have to ask him to leave."

Melody whirled on him, lips tugged to the right once more. "Are you serious? Just delete them."

"Why should I?" He snapped. Perhaps it was the ever-increasing crowd, or perhaps it was the situation's perceived absurdity, but his skin-deep temper was released. "This stuff is here for people to look at! So what if I want to look at it through a lens?"

"This *stuff* is human remains, Ethan." Sharpe was certain the museum attendant was enjoying his wife's muted display of rage. Her scolding's always managed to make him feel like a five-year old whose wall drawings were discovered. "All of this—everything—was once a life. Are you really that disrespectful?"

His pride became buoyant once again. "Right, because creating a museum, hanging body parts up like its *Spirit Halloween,* and letting people gawk at them for eternity is extremely respectful."

"It's for learning!"

Sharpe scoffed. "Right, because that's going *great* for you."

Melody walked away. The crowd parted. As she went up the steps, a choking sob echoed through the open space.

He followed her exit with his gaze as his guilt converted to rage. "I hope you're happy! That wouldn't have happened if you didn't meddle with my business."

The attendant smiled. "I think you should leave now, sir."

Sharpe stomped up the stairs, avoiding the gazes and whispers as he passed. He could hear the click of the woman's heels behind him on the whole ascent. He took a photo of the wall of skulls and the Soap Lady in an act of silent rebellion. His escort said nothing, but a glance over his shoulder showed she stood in the doorway to block him from reentering. At some point between the march from the marble foyer to the wooden doors, his anger was diminished, but the killing blow was seeing Melody on the front steps. Her head was buried in her knees and her shoulders rose and fell with her tears.

Sharpe rubbed a hand across the back of his neck before joining her. His legs stretched out before him and he rested his heels atop the bottom step. His wife's shoulders were clenched, her breath hitched occasionally, and she was hugging her legs. "Mel." He placed a hand on her back. "I think you should go back in."

Melody's head snapped up. Red trails on her cheeks emulated the wisps of flame inside her. "*Should I?* How kind of you to offer."

"I mean it." He removed his hand and placed it on the cool marble step. "I can putz around the city while you look around. You were so excited—"

"I *was* so excited, Ethan, but after that spectacle you made, how do you expect me to go back inside?" Her pause demanded a response, but he couldn't muster one. "You said it was just what you needed. It's just what *I* needed too. You *know* I have a thesis coming up for the board to review, and I thought something here could spark..." Melody shook her head and rose. "Let's just go, okay? We have a long drive home."

She was out of the metal gates and halfway down the sidewalk before Sharpe followed her. It wasn't until they were in the car that they were side-by-side again. She'd taken the passenger seat. His punishment, it seemed, was the three-hour drive home.

He reached for his pocket before he started the car. "Let me try and make it up to you." He opened his camera app and clicked on the Soap Lady's picture in the bottom right corner. He deleted it, and continued the process until all pictures from the museum were gone.

"It's not about the pictures anymore." She leaned her head against the window. When she sighed, condensation clung to it in a misty halo around her face. "But I guess it's a start."

***

The pictures were not actually deleted. *Google Pixel* backed up all pictures to *Google Photos* automatically. When he deleted them from the device, he knew he had something to return to when he got home, even if Melody didn't. His wife locked herself in their room with the dog. Sharpe had only been allowed to grab his pajamas and memory-foam pillow before she began her homemade barricade. His pillow and two of Melody's fleece blankets from the living room now lined the couch in his office. His temporary bed was against the window and across from the door. The far wall was for his bookshelf, and his desk was adjacent to the door. Air buzzed from a vent in the corner. Even without marital disputes, he spent a lot of time in his office. This was especially true when he had a novel to work on.

Melody lived in the world of academic writing. It was insanely tedious to her, but it was an imposed evil necessary for her to get her doctorate. Sharpe operated in the realms of depravity and the darkness of the human experience, at least, he attempted to. Business slowed and his traipsing through the dark dwindled. *Hey buddy* texts and emails from his publisher became more and more frequent. The sales of his previous books were dying out and he needed something else to keep his audience rapt. It was up to his Mütter Museum contraband to satiate his audience's literary blood lust.

Sharpe opened up his laptop. The back of the monitor knocked against a picture frame, which sent at least two knick-knacks toppling over. His desk was only a workspace in a literal sense. He did his work there, true, but the desk was overrun with collectibles, souvenirs, and photographs. Before entertaining the notion of work, he righted his wedding photo, Frankenstein action figure, and Aruba shot glass.

"Alright. Let's get things situated." He opened up *Google Chrome* to get to *Docs*, and another browser to access *Photos*. He found that he got lost easily amongst numerous tabs, and he liked the simplicity of hovering over *Chrome*'s multicolored icon to see everything he had open at once. He opened a third window for emergencies (namely synonym or definition Googling.) He patted his side in search of his *Moleskin* until he realized he was in his pajamas. His red plaid lounge pants had pockets, but they were empty. He switched back to his blank document before rising from his desk.

On his way to the living room, he tried the bedroom door. It was still locked. Percy's growl rumbled. He was likely curled up in Sharpe's spot on the bed, relishing the chance to snuggle with Melody in the vacated space. The dog's warning ceased as soon as he went down the hall. His coat was thrown on the couch amongst the pile of blankets he rummaged through earlier. He flipped through the pages, looking for his most recent entries. *Got it.*

The Soap Lady awaited him on the screen. It was the picture he'd taken. Motion's blur rended the image with its claws, yet her shape was undeniable. He clicked back to *Docs* before resuming his reading. Sharpe didn't register the first *thunk*, but the second grabbed his attention. "Mel, is that you?" He sat in his chair sideways, arm slung across the back.

thunk

"You okay?"

thunk thunk

"Percy?" This hardly sounded like the lab's tail hitting the ground. It was heavy, a sound not unlike when a bowling ball met the lane for the first time. This, however, had an echo to it. "Damn dog."

The Soap Lady greeted him once again. This time, the photo zoomed into her face. Her crud-filled eyes stared through his. He closed the laptop screen quickly.

The sound returned. It was both like and unlike a running faucet at once: it started with a slow trickle, before gaining volume and speed, yet it lacked fluidity and soft sound. *It can't be hail. It sounds like it's inside.* He crossed to the door, listening to the cacophony, mustering the courage to pull it open.

When he did, he saw skulls. They filled his hallway, some piled on the other, but most scattered across the floor with a few inches of space between them. The sound ceased, leaving him in an unfair staring contest until one moved. It tilted toward its chin, almost as if nodding, before hopping into the air and falling upright. Another skull mimicked the front-runner, then another, until their *thunks* were at full capacity once more. They were jumping towards him.

Sharpe slammed the door shut and pressed his back against it. His feet slid away from him, and he locked his knees. As they hit the door, it shook, yet they got no further. "They don't have hands," he laughed. He turned to watch the door. Their efforts only served to make it shiver. "Take that, you glorified rocks!"

The crying began. It was high pitched and desperate, wailing without reprieve. The vent lid popped into the air, its fall muted against the carpet, drowned out by the screams. A small, plaster hand appeared first. Tiny fingers gripped at the fabric. The baby's head and other arm hoisted up from the vent. Its sorrow filled the room and echoed off the vents as it dragged itself forward. Swinging its arms outwards and forwards as it sped into the room. Helpless legs flailed at the hips, kicking aimlessly and uselessly at the air before the lower hands and head came out. The casted infant moved on its four hands with its heads lulling to the ground and sides, screeching all the while. It lumbered towards him.

Sharpe's knees threatened to buckle when he grabbed the doorknob. On one side, he had an army of skulls. On the other, a spider-crawling plaster baby. He wasn't given the option to decide between the two, because the door swung open. The Giant's skeleton had to duck to get into the room. He'd always thought skeletal villains in movies were corny. It was the least gory version of the dead he could think of, and he'd always imagined that movement would appear ungainly at best. When faced with his own mortal infrastructure, however, he was less certain of his incredulousness. "Now, wait a minute—"

The bone figure lifted the author. Sharpe punched right between the skeleton's ribs. His knuckles bled from scraping against the bone. The Giant put Sharpe down in his swivel chair and took the human's stuck hand by the wrist to gently pull it out. Some of the skulls dared to venture into the room. One was being used by the baby as a drum. Another bumped into the couch and toppled over. Those that stayed in the hallway began to part. The Soap Lady had arrived.

At first, Sharpe could only make out her silhouette by the trickles of moonlight that highlighted his living room. As she drew closer, she melded with the darkness, reforming only when reaching the fingers of artificial light from his office. Her movements were fluid in spite of her captivity. The Soap Lady held a presence through the sheer weight of her existence. *Look*, she seemed to say, *at what you might become, at what you* will *become*. He shuddered. The Giant held him firm until the unnamed woman stood before him.

"I…If you are here because of the pictures, I can—" His response was cut off by her hand clamping over his mouth. Her smell rested atop his skin, burrowed into his nose. With her grip, she tilted his head upward to force Sharoe to look into her non-existent eyes, to acknowledge her scream. She placed a hand on his chest. The muck spread like moisture on cotton candy. It was a webbed, rippling movement. The substance, somehow slimy and dry at once, took over. He could feel it blanket his body, his extremities, before slowly rising to his head. The Soap Lady's head tilted further to the side, almost at a ninety-degree angle. As he tried to scream, the muck poured down his throat. She kept eye contact with him until his face was fully covered. Sharpe screamed again and gargled his own decay.

"Ethan!"

The writer opened his eyes to see his office draped in sunlight. He was on the floor beside his couch, his wife leaning over him. "Mel?"

"Are you okay? I heard you screaming."

"I guess I just had a bad dream."

"Well, that's called *karma*." Melody stood up. "Meet me in the kitchen for breakfast. *You're* cooking, but since you had a hard night, I'll make the coffee."

"Yeah, okay. I'll be right out." He crossed to his desk. The laptop was open. He put his hand on the track pad and screamed. His knuckles were still bloody.

Dog Days

Bruno's tongue curled out to Stacy's hand through his jowls. Gray polluted his black fur, forcing it to compete for the harsh, fluorescent light amongst overburdening weeds. His eyes were smudged with a gray film, like milk poured over coffee: cloudy, spectral, overpowering.

The stainless-steel table below him channeled the chills from Stacy's spine. Her eyes clouded too, but precipitation cured them, the tears forming puddles by Bruno's paws. A patch of fur was shaved off the right one, an IV awaiting the vets' return. Stacy's smile lied. "It's going to be okay, bubba."

Knock, knock.

Stacy lowered to her knees. As the door closed behind the intruder, she pressed her nose to his muzzle, so that she could look into his eyes. "I'm right here, bub. I've gotcha."

"He can feel your emotions. Try to keep a smile."

The advice was cruel. *How can I smile? How can I not?* Love, they say, makes people capable of anything. It helps moms lift cars off their babies, spouses rush into burning buildings, pet owners smile in the face of death. "Remember when I brought you home?" Stacy felt the vet looming over her shoulder. Every muscle in her body strained against the urge to push the doctor away, to stop them, but Bruno's soft eyes stopped her. *It's what's best for him.* "I called everyone I knew. I said, 'Come look at my handsome boy!' And they came. Do you remember that?"

Bruno's tongue lopped out.

"First needle now." The vet's voice rang in a swan song.

"I love you. I love you so much. Never forget that, bubba."

Something changed in Bruno's eyes. A shadow passed through; a curtain slid shut. He was no longer there.

"Now for the second."

Stacy couldn't make herself leave. Her head stayed on his. His left paw stretched out and locked onto her. His right paw did the same and both sets of nails dug down into her shoulder.

"They have spasms sometimes." The vet sounded bored. "He can't feel it, I promise."

Stacy wanted to kick them, but Bruno needed her. His paw retracted and bolted out again, as if he was flailing beneath the surface, begging his mom for help. Movement stopped all together as his head flopped to the side.

"It's done." Stacy felt the hand on her shoulder. It was gentle, but the vet's smile made it feel condescending. "I'm so sorry for your loss."

Stacy felt a million curses boil in her throat. *She killed my Bruno, my bubba.* "Yeah."

"Would you like us to cremate him? Or would you like to bury him?"

The thought of Bruno home, but not *there* made her stomach churn. Burning him didn't sound any better. "Can I decide later?"

"Sure. We'll keep him in the fridge for the day. Call us when you decide."

Bruno hated the cold. In the winter, he would curl up with his SpongeBob blanket on the couch. In the summer, he would lay on his side, his fur sparkling in the sunlight. "Okay, thanks." *I hate this place. I hate everyone here. So, so much.* This mantra repeated until she reached the car. Her head parked on the wheel as internal suffering ousted itself. Tears painted her cheeks, screams pounded against her own eardrums.

Patrons walked by with their spry pups and cat carriers. Why would they bring their pets near her, rub her nose in grief? As they passed by, many rubbernecked at the display. They would shake their heads and frown. They saw inevitability.

***

John was waiting on the front porch for Stacy as she pulled into the driveway. He was seated on the top step, his *Gritstones* just below the rest of him. The shallow staircase made it look as though he'd adopted the fetal position, his jeans to his chest, pressed against his hoodie. His puffy eyes, red cheeks, and swollen bottom lip further sold the look of a baby on the verge of breakdown. In spite of this, he smiled at her. It was a perfunctory smile, one reserved for unhappy occasions. "I'm sorry I couldn't be there, Stace."

This turn had come so suddenly and with John working so far away, she knew he wasn't at fault. Resentment boiled in her chest regardless. *How could he* not *be there* gnawed at the back of her skull. She collapsed on the steps next to him, docking her head on his shoulder. His stubble tickled her temple. "I just want my bubba back."

He turned to kiss her head. Dirty blond hair jabbed her in the eye. "He was a good dog. But he's in a better place now, y'know?"

John became repulsive. Stacy retreated accordingly. "How do *you* know?"

He responded with a hand to her back which she scooted away from.

"He's in a freezer. That doesn't sound like a better place to me."

"A… Why is he—"

"We have to decide whether we want to bury him here or cremate him." John's silence choked her. Instead of answering, he rubbed circles along the brick steps with his thumb. "I want him home, John."

"Okay, sure. If you wanna pick him up, I can start digging a hole in the backyard. Maybe under his tree?"

There was a God-knows-what kind of tree in their backyard. It wasn't tall, as trees went, maybe only eight feet. It produced pink flowers in the spring. Toward the end of the summer, the petals would start to sprinkle down and stick to Bruno like glitter. He would often scratch his back on a root. Occasionally, he would lay his head against the trunk as he took a nap.

"I don't want to go back there."

John's shoulders pressed to his ears and never dropped. "You wanna start digging then?"

Stacy mimicked his earlier fetal position, only her face buried into her knees. A waterfall of dark hair draped over the front of them. This time, when John placed a hand on her back, she didn't reject it.

"I'll be back, okay?' He rubbed his hand up and down her spine. "Love you."

"Lub you too." Stacy's lips, pressed against her legs, made it sound like she was talking through wool. "Bring his blanket. It's in my backseat." She felt John's leg press against her side as he stood. He took her hand in his so that he could get to the keys underneath. A mechanical *beep beep* heralded his departure and the crackle of rubber against rocks confirmed it.

His return held no fanfare. SpongeBob cheered the couple on as they made their solemn procession to the backyard. The frozen ground required a pickax to loosen the soil. Stacy watched as John lowered the fleece bundle into the earth. The lump under SpongeBob's watchful eyes offered no solace, no movement. The first clump blocked out his open smile. The smell of dirt and cold made her throat sting with tears. She retreated back to the house, all the while hearing the slushing of earth behind her.

The howling wind scratching at the window awoke Stacy from her sleep. John lay on his side, back to her, unperturbed by the outdoor commotion. She pulled the cotton throw blanket with her as she went over to the window. The tree's branches cast a claw across the lawn under the moonlight. The wind recoiled from the glass, whistling as it whipped by. *My poor bubba. All alone in the cold.* Stacy tied the corners of the blanket around her neck in a makeshift cloak. She slipped on her *Ugg* slippers and threw open her bedroom door. She half expected to see Bruno blocking the doorway, lifting his head in a question, but was greeted by bare wooden floors.

The wind billowed her blanket like fresh linens on a clothesline as she stepped into the backyard. The dirt tossed onto Bruno's grave was already starting to harden in the January chill. Tomorrow it would take a strained effort to reach her dog. The grass wet her knees, its blades stabbing through fleece pajama bottoms. She let a hand fall to the soil and lifted a clump. *How long will it take for Bruno to be dirt?* Her eyes congested with tears. She tossed it over her shoulder. Then some more. And more. She found SpongeBob's smile first, then his eyes. The rest appeared like a mirage—a piece here and there before it all came together.

"I'm sorry, bubba. I'm sorry it's not warmer."

SpongeBob answered with his open-mouthed laugh. Stacy covered his face with her hand but drew back quickly. The blanket was a mixture of sand and moist cotton. The mass of fur and bones below was a block of ice—immobile, cold, and hard. Sentiment blinded her more than tears.

"Do you wanna come inside?"

Bruno remained silent.

"You wanna get toasty warm?" A clump of dirt tumbled from the side and atop her hand. She shook it off. "Just for tonight, okay?" Stacy leaned over the bundle, scooping her arms below. Bruno rolled to her chest as she pulled, staying pressed against her as she lifted up. Stacy placed him on the rim of his grave to wait while she kicked the dirt back into place. The dirt settled just below where it originally was, making a pothole in the grass. "Daddy won't mind, bubba." Stacy hoisted the bundle to her chest again. She could feel his head lull over her arm in a morbid *Dirty Dancing* parody. "Or maybe we'll keep this our little secret. Sound good?"

Stacy held the door open with her foot, which she shifted to her shoulder as she wedged herself inside, then to her back as she eased the door shut. "Now where to put you?"

Bruno loved sleeping in front of the fireplace on his plush doggie-bed. His head would nestle on the side closest to the fire as his tail swept the carpet behind him. *John would see him there.* He often nestled between them in bed, the back of his head pressed against Stacy's shoulder, legs parallel to push John to the bed's edge. *He's a deep sleeper but when he wakes up... God, he'd be so mad at Bruno.* Down in the basement, Bruno would lean his back against the boiler room door as she did laundry, enjoying the makeshift summer air that seeped through.

"You've never been in there, right? Too many wires." Stacy started toward the steps. Only one of the basement lights was connected to a light switch. This was at the very top of the stairs, which meant you had to walk down into the void until you could feel the beaded, metal string whack you in the forehead. She climbed down into the dark maw. Her weight shifted back on her heels, toes gripping the steps' edges like birds on a cable line. Stacy had to pin Bruno to her chest as she pulled on the cord. There were boxes pushed against the far-left wall, filled with holiday decorations. A plastic Santa leaned on a forty-five-degree angle against a box marked "Christmas Tree." The washer and dryer were in the middle of the back wall. The boiler room was on the opposite end of the decorations. There was no lightbulb in that room. Light came from the moonlight through low, rectangular windows that had long since lost its wire mesh guard. Stacy put Bruno down right in the doorway. He already felt less hard, less cold. "This'll do you good, bubba. Just for tonight, okay?"

People say that to dogs under many different circumstances: eating from the table, sleeping in the bed, lying on the couch. Just like those instances, Bruno's occupancy of the boiler room lasted longer than one night. Dogs are masters of persuasion. Stacy would sneak downstairs when John left for his morning shifts. The dangers of construction weren't limited to hazardous tools. The perils included 4am drives with coffee as the only life preserver. This left Stacy with a few hours to sit with her dog until she had to prepare for work. She would lean her boyfriend's pillow against the wall and stroke her hand down the blanket. Bruno was warm: warm and soft. She often felt her hand sink down into him like memory foam as she stroked his side. She never took the blanket off of him, though she longed to scratch behind his ears, to rub his belly, which he would present with kicked back legs like an award. The blanket trapped in the smell. The blanket protected her image of Bruno.

Until it didn't.

Lavender *Febreze* did nothing to cut through the stench. Bruno was squishy. His blanket began to stick to him, an unidentifiable liquid occasionally seeping through. When touched, Bruno sounded like a squeezed sponge.

"Maybe you need to cool off." Stacy rubbed her hand against the concrete floor. It greeted her skin like sandpaper. "What do you think?"

Ooze came through the blanket in a lake of unidentifiable slime. Stacy stood, stepped over her dog, and tried to lift the window's latch. It was stuck. She had to push with her palm until it parted. Cool, unimpeded air collected in the room.

"Cool off for a while. I'll be back, Bruno, I just need to wash my hands, okay?"

She closed the door behind her.

Creeeek.

Stacy looked upward. The upstairs floorboard objected to someone's presence. *Didn't John already leave?* She went for the steps. "Babe?" *Creek.* The steps moved for the basement. "Babe, is that you?"

John poked his head through the doorway. "You're up early, Stace."

She ascended to join her husband, who had since retreated back to the kitchen. She made it just in time to watch him pour his *ShopRite* half-and-half into his *Dixie* to-go cup. Hazelnut laced the air. "Aren't you supposed to be on your way?"

"What? Trying to get rid of me?" John's brow and the corner of his lip raised in tandem. "That's not very nice, y'know."

"Of course not. Just wondering what's wrong."

"I see." He made a vague gesture to his jeans. She was tempted to guess a pattern out of the newly made stain. "Spilled my coffee when

I was getting in the truck. I'll be damned if I do that drive without it."

"That sucks." The stain looked like a giraffe — thin and long before dissolving into a long brick. "Sorry, babe."

"Yeah, me too." He turned to put the lid on his cup. "What about you, babe? Why are you up so early?"

"I'm okay. I just threw a blanket in the dryer downstairs."

"Why?"

"It's pretty cold."

"Why don't you just turn off the fan?"

"That's not as comfy as a warm blanket."

"Fair." John turned back around, the cup to his lips. "By the way, babe, before I go, have you noticed a like…" His lips hugged as he searched for the right words. "*Smell?*"

Stacy's lips mimicked his. "What kind of smell?"

"A gross one. Like spoiled milk and boiled fish had a baby."

"Maybe it's a skunk?"

"Yeah, maybe." He moved toward her, placing a peck on her lips. She could taste the hazelnut. "I'll check it out when I get home. Love you."

"Love you, too. Have fun at work."

The door punctuated John's exit. It vibrated through the air like bass in a good song, making her ears buzz. He was going to find Bruno later, find him and make him go outside. *I have to move him. Just for a little while, then he can come back. He won't mind.*

As she descended, her mind raced with options. John would likely search the attic. Under the bed was too obvious.

Maybe he won't mind the shed?

This was the safest option. The smell would be out of the house long enough for John to forget about it. The shed, used for extra storage space, was mostly forgotten about. He'd never go in there.

"Bubba! Wanna go outside?"

Click-clack.

Stacy paused.

Click-clack.

It sounded like nails along the concrete floor. She'd heard it many times as he patrolled the basement, sniffing corners, inspecting shadows.

Scritchscritchscritch

"Bruno? Bruno, my bubba-lubba. Outside?" She flung open the

boiler room door. To her chagrin, he wasn't waiting at the door for her, tongue lulled to the side, ears perked up. He remained hidden under the bundle, yet something was different— there was movement. There was a soft *thup thup* against the ground that made Stacy smile. "You *do* wanna go outside? Good boy! Whosah good boy?"

thup thup

Stacy took SpongeBob's eyes in her hands and pulled. Bruno flopped to the floor. A scream gagged her and refused to leave her throat. Her eyes watered in a trickle before the dam burst loose.

Bruno's fur looked like a throw rug draped over whatever was left of him. A rib poked through. His jowls were pulled back from his jaws. Maggots took that as an invitation to explore his teeth. A pool of cherry jello coated the inside of the blanket, but some of it fell onto the floor in chunks. One eyeball was gone, another was deflated in the socket. By his tail was a rat, who gnawed through it, scavenging the bones. There was no blood, only ooze. The rat continued with its feast, ignorant or apathetic to Stacy's presence.

"Get away from him!"

The rat, who never learned human speech, continued.

Stacy's foot met the rat's head again and again. The forced introduction spread blood all over the walls, all over the boiler, all over Bruno.

That's not Bruno. The scream released its gag order in choked sobs. Bruno was gone, gone, gone and there was nothing she could do for him. Nothing but put him to rest.

Epilogue From The Raven Master

The Raven Master marks their page with a black feather. "Dawn is approaching." *Instead of replacing the book on the shelf, he leaves it on the seat for them to continue when night entices once again. The ravens follow only after the door is open, guided by lamplight until they return to the museum. The yeomen would soon awaken. Few know of the birds' nightly sojourn outside of superstition, and mortal knowledge would only hamper their proceedings. The absence of their charges therefore remained a secret between orator, flock, and the gloom.*

The unkindness flits up into the moonlight, abandoning their ward until the following night. He hangs the lantern on a hook by the stairs and proceeds into the darkness. It is for their benefit, not his, that the way is lit. The passage is ingrained in his every movement, inscribed in every footstep. Echoes of footfall replace the flutter of wings and imitative coos.

The air hardens as he steps into the catacomb. Every particle is laced with decay and nitre. His predestined path brings him back to his grave. The story-teller's gloved hand runs along his enclosure's edge before he slides into place. Mold hangs down in vines above his form. He stares into the void above him, all around him, searching for his contemporaries. "It's humorous, is it not? We are given a lordly title, indeed, even a place of honor, yet it is our charges who hold power." *Dawn encroaches above the walls. It is then he will join the fallen in their repose until the flock demands his duty be carried out once again. He chuckles with the last of his will.* "I wonder, then, my friends, if we really *are* the masters here."

Acknowledgements

This is the hardest part of this book to write. Before I became a serious writer, I was very guilty of ignoring this part. Frankly, I thought it would only be of interest to the people mentioned or serve as a sort of professional obligation. To be fair, this isn't *wrong*, but it is hard to ignore the sentiment behind each name. Writing is portrayed as a solitary career, and yet, there are so many people who support writers behind the scenes that deserve credit.

The first thank you has to go to my family. My parents, grandparents, siblings, aunts and uncles, cousins, the list goes on. Each and every one of you needs to know how important you are to me and how happy I am to have you as my cheerleaders. I have this joke that my Mom-Mom serves as my sole marketing executive in southwest Florida. My mom bought 30 books from *Dark Matter Magazine* to lob at people. They all have supported me immeasurably. There is no way I can repay them and there is nothing to say other than thank you, I love you.

Nan, who this book is dedicated to, has been my writing mentor since I was thirteen-years-old. She was a teen librarian in my library system at the time and was promoting her book *Hiding Out at the Pancake Palace.* The volunteer coordinator pushed me to talk to her. Although I was terrified, we struck up a conversation, and from that, a writing club was born. Nan has been so supportive of me every step of the way, even when I presented stories I still cringe to look at today. I was bullied all throughout middle and high school, but the writing club and Nan's support gave me something to fall back on. An outlet. Hope. I know you'll never agree with this, Nan, but you're one of the reasons I am where I am today.

I get by with a little help from my friends. There is no way I can ignore their help and impact. The first person I need to thank is E. Blaze Stark, who proofread 99% of these stories to ensure they were up to snuff. He's a fantastic writer who has an incredibly successful comic book writing career ahead of him. Gavin Gardiner was my first writing friend. He introduced me to the horror writing community on social media and I am beyond grateful for his friendship and virtual mentorship. If you haven't read *For Rye*, you're doing yourself a disservice. There are countless (I mean this very literally) people I could thank in the virtual writing world. L.R.J. Allen and Wofford Lee Jones are probably the earliest of my connections, so I want to say a thank you to them. I also have my real-life writing friends, Emma, Rachel, Sam, Patrick, Julia, Alfredo, and Damien who have acted as a sounding board for me over the years." Of course, I have my non-writing friends, Alexa, Jo-El, Ed, Alex, and Sean that have supported my writing throughout the years as well. I am so happy you all put up with me.

"Shock" was pulled from the "Human Monsters" submissions and given to *Dark Matter Magazine* for their second Halloween edition. Rob Carroll and the *DMM* team took a chance on me for my first publication, and I will never forget it. *Shortwave Publishing* also pulled me from the "OBSOLESCENCE" submission pile to include in their online magazine. Alan Lastufka is owed thanks for his support and friendship throughout the process of publishing "Portrait of an Artist." My friends at *Poe Boy Publishing* found me in a video where I unboxed my *DMM* Halloween edition, crying like a baby. They asked me for the first two stories in my collection shortly thereafter. When I got the email that this collection would be published, I ran around the library I work at, sobbing, calling everyone I knew to inform them that I finally made it: I have a book. Graeme, Derek, Carole and Hache - this whole collection is possible because of you. Thank you so much for all of your support, guidance, and encouragement.

A very special thanks goes out to all of my beta readers as well. Kiera, Lauren K., E.F. Deal, Lauren Carter, Josh, Charlie, Brandon Grafius, Jay Bechtol, and L.R.J. Allen, thank you, thank you for helping me make this work the best it can be."

Last, but certainly not least, I want to thank you, dear reader. You picked up my very first book and that is a brave thing to do. You never know how these debut writings will turn out, but, if you have read this far, I am assuming you liked it? I hope you did, but even if you didn't, thanks for the support. Readers are an author's lifeblood. We are nothing without you. Look forward to more frights and screams, kiddos.

The Raven Master will return…

…You have been warned.

www.ingramcontent.com/pod-product-compliance
Lightning Source LLC
Chambersburg PA
CBHW030615310726
48979CB00003B/726